HUW POWELL

BLOOMSBURY
NEW YORK   LONDON   NEW DELHI   SYDNEY

First published in Great Britain in July 2014
by Bloomsbury Publishing Plc
Published in the United States of America in June 2015
by Bloomsbury Children's Books
www.bloomsbury.com

Bloomsbury is a registered trademark of Bloomsbury Publishing Plc

For information about permission to reproduce selections from
this book, write to Permissions, Bloomsbury Children's Books,
1385 Broadway, New York, New York 10018
Bloomsbury books may be purchased for business
or promotional use. For information on bulk purchases
please contact Macmillan Corporate and Premium Sales Department
at specialmarkets@macmillan.com

Library of Congress Cataloging-in-Publication Data
Powell, Huw.
Spacejackers / by Huw Powell.
        pages   cm
Summary: As a baby, Jake Cutler was separated from his family
and left on the planet Remota, deep in the seventh solar system.
Eleven years later, Jake carries a secret within himself that could
change the entire universe. Jake must discover the truth about his past
before he is hunted down and caught by ruthless space pirates.
ISBN 978-1-61963-515-9 (hardcover) • ISBN 978-1-61963-516-6 (e-book)
[1. Science fiction. 2. Adventure and adventurers—Fiction. 3. Identity—Fiction.
4. Pirates—Fiction.] I. Title.
PZ7.1.P69Sp 2015   [Fic]—dc23   2014021480

Typeset by Hewer Text UK Ltd., Edinburgh
Printed and bound in the U.S.A. by Thomson-Shore Inc., Dexter, Michigan
2 4 6 8 10 9 7 5 3 1

For my son, Cadan

Prologue

A Stranger in the Storm

Deep in the seventh solar system lurked Remota, a gray and desolate planet with a split personality. During the day conditions on Remota were hot and dry, but at night fierce storms would lash its craggy continents. Few people ventured outside after dark, which is why no one noticed a wounded figure staggering through the space docks late one evening.

A particularly nasty storm gripped Remota that night. Wild streaks of lightning ripped across the sky, while furious bursts of thunder shook the ground. The stranger stumbled as he fought through acid rain and ice-cold winds, but he lurched onward, shielding his bloodied face with a ragged cloak.

The nearest shelter was an old monastery on Temple Hill, where a group of cyber-monks dedicated their lives to studying technology. It was a solid structure built of local stone, with great wooden entrance doors and stained-glass windows protected beneath metal storm hatches. Its single tower was encrusted with satellite dishes and topped with a pulsing beacon to warn away ships that were forced to land in the space docks at night.

The stranger paused at the foot of the hill to catch his breath. His weary eyes traced a crude path through the rocks and fixed on the secluded monastery at the top. He stared at it for a moment, focusing on his goal, and then he began to climb.

Father Pius Gates hurried along the main corridor, his leather sandals slapping against the smooth flagstones and his black robes trailing in the darkness. The cyber-abbot was a large man with gray hair and a face that had drooped with age. At the end of the corridor, the front door buzzed like an angry electronic insect.

"Hold on, hold on," he muttered. "I'm coming."

"Open up," pleaded an unfamiliar voice.

The cyber-monks were not used to visitors and they were wary of strangers. Remota was an independent colony with little in the way of law enforcement. There had been recent reports of space pirate raids on the edge of the seventh solar system, not that anyone on Remota had anything worth stealing. Mostly farmers had settled there, growing rare and exotic plants that fed on acid rain.

Father Pius reached the door and activated a small video screen. It flickered into life to reveal a lone man standing in the shadows. The cyber-abbot squinted at the display. As far as he could tell, the visitor was neither a farmer nor a dockworker, but he did appear to be clutching something inside his cloak.

"Who is it?" asked Father Pius into the video com. "What do you want?"

"Help us," pleaded the stranger, speaking with an unusual clipped accent that the cyber-abbot did not recognize. "Our ship was destroyed in a space storm and our escape pod landed on your planet. We desperately need shelter and medical attention."

"We?" said Father Pius warily. "I don't understand. I can see only you. Who else is there?"

The man opened his cloak, revealing a young boy, no more than two years old, wrapped in an orange blanket. The child clung to the man's chest and shook with each new rumble of thunder.

Father Pius unlocked the door and pulled back the thick metal hatches. "Quick, come in where it's warm," he said. "Remota is no place for a child at night."

The stranger limped forward and handed the boy to the cyber-abbot. "His name is Jake Cutler," he said, and instead of entering the monastery himself, he stepped back and gazed into the sky. "We were hit by asteroids. It all happened so fast. We were lucky to escape with our lives. I don't think anyone else survived."

The stranger's burned cloak flapped behind him like blackened wings. Father Pius didn't recognize his maroon uniform, but the rows of medals suggested that he was some kind of military officer. The emblem on his chest was a gold disk containing three small circles, one white, one red, and one green. There were three deep cuts on the man's forehead.

"You're injured," said Father Pius.

"I'm not important. You must help the boy. His father was lost in the space storm."

"Lost? You mean he went down with the ship?"

"No, we became separated and he was unable to reach the escape pods. He found a space suit and evacuated through the air lock, but we lost contact with him. If Jake's father somehow avoided being crushed to death in the asteroid field, he would have run out of air by now. The boy has nobody left."

"What about his mother?"

"She died giving birth to him almost two years ago. Jake is alone and vulnerable, and he needs a home."

"This isn't an orphanage," protested Father Pius, guessing where the conversation was heading.

"I'm sorry, but Jake is in danger as long as he stays with me." The man backed away from the door. "You must help him. He's very special."

Father Pius glanced down at the child and was startled to see two vacant eyes staring back.

"His eyes . . . ?"

"They were damaged by a leaking fuel cell," said the stranger. "Is there anything you can do to help?"

"I don't know, but I'll take a look."

Father Pius struggled to protect Jake from the acid rain as it spattered off the door frame.

"Please, come inside," he said. "Let me dress your wounds and fetch you some clean clothes. We have plenty of spare robes."

"No, I must leave now before I put Jake in any more danger." The man stepped farther away. "Don't trust anyone who comes looking for him. His life depends on it."

Father Pius wondered why anyone would want to hurt an innocent child. He explored Jake's face and noticed a gold pendant hanging from a chain around his neck. It had a swirling round border encircling three precious stones: a diamond, a ruby, and an emerald.

"What's this?" he asked.

"Keep it safe," said the stranger. "It's the key to his past." Then he turned and headed away down the hill through the corrosive rain.

Father Pius strained his eyes to keep sight of the man, but he was gone. The cyber-abbot might have chased after him, if it hadn't been for the small boy shivering in his arms. Instead, he retreated inside and closed the door, unsure what to make of the situation.

"Who are you, Jake Cutler?" he whispered.

Jake didn't make a sound as he lay trembling in the cyber-abbot's arms. His eyes stared blankly into the darkness where the stranger had stood moments before, but all that remained was the small video screen, which flickered a few times and turned itself off.

Chapter 1

The Visitor

"Watch out below!" cried Jake Cutler, sliding down the banister of the main staircase, his thick brown hair blowing across his bright purple eyes.

The cyber-monks had restored Jake's sight following the space storm eleven years ago, replacing his irises with special computerized lenses that were powered by blinking. His vision had been good ever since, better than average, but it meant that his eyes glowed luminous purple, sparkling like precious amethysts set in balls of expensive china.

Jake spiraled past several surprised cyber-monks in gray robes, before leaping off the end of the banister and landing nimbly on his feet. He adjusted his backpack and checked the clock on the wall.

"Magnifty!" he cheered. "A new record."

Before the cyber-monks could catch up, Jake was sprinting along the corridor to the front door, where Father Pius Gates had just returned from the local market.

"Jake Cutler," said the cyber-abbot, removing his protective sunglasses. He had a neat row of five studs across his forehead. These were special implants that enabled the cyber-monks to control computers with their thoughts. "How many times do I have to tell you? No running in the monastery."

"Sorry, Father. It won't happen again."

"It had better not. I have only a few gray hairs left and I would like to keep them, thank you very much." Father Pius was still one of the youngest cyber-abbots in the galaxy at the age of sixty. He eyed Jake suspiciously. "Where are you heading in such haste?"

"I'm going down to the space docks to watch the ships land." Jake slipped on his sunglasses and stepped through the doorway. "Brother Jonas said I could finish my studies tonight."

Father Pius had no time to object before Jake had broken into a run and was disappearing down the hill.

"Stay out of trouble," he called after him. "And don't talk to strangers."

Jake enjoyed spending time in the space docks. It was much more exciting than the stuffy monastery and there was always something new to see. In the last five years, Remota had transformed from a small farming planet into a thriving trade world. Large corporations had invested in expensive drilling equipment to mine the surface for crystals and other minerals. New towns had replaced the old settlements, and there was a constant flow of space traffic to and from the extended space docks.

Spacecraft landed at the old steel jetties that jutted into the sky like giant fingers, or at the modern dome-shaped terminals that were designed for passenger ships and space tankers. In the sunlight, these impressive platforms glistened like enormous glass bubbles and were surrounded by an assortment of shops, cafés, and restaurants. There was even a stall selling souvenirs for tourists.

Jake would often stay there for hours, sitting in the shade and drinking apple juice, while he sketched spacecraft and dreamed of distant worlds. He would talk to the pilots and crews, asking them questions about their ships and home planets. They would tell him exciting stories about giant monsters and fearsome pirates, which fueled his imagination. Jake didn't count these spacefarers as strangers; not really.

"Hello, Orana," he said, approaching the dock gates.

"Hi there, Jakester." The security guard greeted

him, leaning out of her cabin window. "What are you going to draw today?"

"I'm hoping to see that pleasure cruiser from Reus again." Jake opened his backpack and pulled out a sketch of an expensive-looking spacecraft, with the name *Star Chaser* written on the side. "The copilot said they would be back this week."

"Hey, that's your best drawing yet."

"Thanks! What I really want to see is a naval warship. Do you think one will ever land here?"

"Sorry, sweetie, you know the Interstellar Navy isn't welcome on Remota, or any other independent colony for that matter."

No one seemed to like the Interstellar Navy, not even the cyber-monks. People referred to them as the "Fascist Fleet." It was something to do with politics. There were tensions between the Interstellar Government, who ruled the United Worlds, and the independent colonies, but that didn't interest Jake. He just liked the smart naval uniforms and powerful warships.

"Maybe you'll get to see one in space some day," said Orana, throwing him an apple and opening the gates. "In the meantime, if you help me to fix my hover-bike later, I'll give you another flying lesson in the security shuttle."

Jake thanked her and walked into the main concourse, with its familiar parade of shops that sold everything from sunblock to space suits. In the distance, the jetties and terminals towered high above the rooftops. He had seen hundreds of spaceships come and go over the years, but entering the docks never failed to excite him.

Jake knew everything there was to know about space. He just hadn't seen it for himself. There was a whole galaxy waiting to be explored, but Father Pius wouldn't let him leave Remota, let alone the seventh solar system. Jake longed for adventure. He dreamed of blasting off on a rugged pirate ship and searching for treasure. A few months ago, he had even attempted to stow away on a supply craft, only to be caught and returned to the monastery.

Apart from his secret fantasy about becoming a swashbuckling space pirate, Jake wanted to enlist with the Interstellar Navy and travel the seven solar systems. Not that he had mentioned this to Father Pius, who hoped that Jake would become a novice before one day taking his cyber-monk vows.

After the rise of the virtual religions a hundred years ago, the cyber-cults were formed. Thousands of people across the galaxy now studied and worshipped technology. The cyber-monks on Remota were in the order of Codos, who believed that technology could unlock the mysteries of the universe, such as time travel and teleportation. This was only theoretical, of course, because despite years of research, they had yet to make a significant discovery. But Jake couldn't imagine wearing gray hooded robes and having studs implanted in his skull, like Father Pius.

He didn't mean to cause trouble, but he couldn't help feeling that he was supposed to be somewhere else, other than on Remota. It wasn't easy growing up not knowing who your parents were or where you came from, or why you had been dumped in a monastery on a secluded planet. The one question that haunted Jake the most was whether or not his father had survived the space storm all those years ago.

"Are you up there, Dad?" he asked the sky. "Are you coming to get me?"

Jake climbed onto a broken cargo crate and opened his backpack. He rummaged inside the bag and pulled out a section of orange cloth, cut from his old blanket. Apart from the gold pendant, the piece of blanket was all that he had left from his past, and though it was little more than a tattered rag now, it was one of the things he treasured most. He rubbed the cloth in his fingers and breathed its comforting scent, trying to remember how it had once smelled.

As he sat there, something furry leaped onto the crate and sniffed his backpack.

"Hello, Hacks," said Jake. "Sorry, no food in there today, unless you want some of my apple."

Hacks was a spotted ginger cat, with a mangled tail and a half-chewed ear, who lived in the space docks. Nobody seemed to own him, but Orana always left out water and food scraps. Jake had named him Hacks because of the noise he made when coughing up dust.

"I'll bring you some cake next week."

It was almost Jake's birthday, his least favorite day of the year. He was going to be thirteen, but nobody knew the actual date he was born, so the cyber-monks celebrated the anniversary of his arrival instead. For Jake, that would always be the night he was abandoned.

Hacks curled up on the warm crate and purred, while Jake tucked the orange cloth back into his bag and took out his drawing materials. A long-distance passenger ship had just docked in one of the terminals, and he was keen to draw it while the crew refueled. He quickly sketched the outline of the hull as people swarmed from the terminal exit.

Most of them were crystal miners arriving for their shifts, but there were also new farmhands, traveling salesmen, and the occasional tourist.

A tall man with dark wavy hair appeared in the crowd, his mirrored glasses reflecting the bright sunlight. There was something about him that made him stand out from the other passengers. Perhaps it was the confident way he walked or his strange-looking clothes. He wore a faded red shirt with brass fasteners, tight denim trousers, and designer leather boots. In his hands he carried a flask of water and a long blue coat. A few steps behind, a shorter man with curly red hair dragged an overfilled bag.

The tall man stopped to drink some water and check his wrist computer. He turned in the street and pointed to the monastery on Temple Hill, which seemed to please his stocky friend, who nodded in approval. After a brief discussion, the tall man set off toward the dock gates on his own, his blue coat draped over his shoulder.

Jake stuffed his things back into his pack and hopped off the crate. It looked as though the cyber-monks had a visitor and Jake wanted to find out why.

Over the years Jake had read countless tales of space-jacking and swashbuckling, starring such famous pirate captains as James Hawker and Scarabus Shark. He knew they were the bad guys, but he still found their adventures thrilling. What would it be like to fire a laser cannon or board an enemy craft? It was his dream to be a hero in a battle, beating the odds and emerging victorious. Perhaps it was this sense of adventure that made him follow the man with the blue coat.

Jake knew every inch of Temple Hill. He scurried from rock to rock, taking care not to be seen by the stranger. His mind was burning with curiosity. The cyber-monks rarely had guests, only new recruits or the occasional messenger from the cardinal, but never anyone wearing mirrored glasses and designer boots.

At the top of the hill, the man stopped to take in the view. Jake ducked out of sight and waited a moment, before peering out from behind his rock. The stranger was now at the monastery's main entrance and talking with the novice who had opened the door, but they were too far away to hear. How could Jake get closer without being seen? Then it struck him; whenever there had been visitors in the past, they had all met with the head of the monastery first, Father Pius.

Jake sprinted along the outside of the monastery

to the cyber-abbot's office. The window was always open during the day because of the heat, which meant that Jake would be able to hear any conversation inside. He crept the last few steps and crouched beneath the window ledge, listening intently.

"Thank you, Bernsley," said Father Pius, dismissing the novice.

Jake heard the door close and the sound of dust being brushed from clothes. He risked a peek through the window and saw the stranger hanging up his long blue coat. The man had removed his mirrored sunglasses and his deep blue eyes were fixed on Father Pius. He had one of those familiar faces, except for a strong chin and a nose that had been broken at least once. Jake noticed two metal studs fixed to the sides of his head, similar to the skull implants used by the cyber-monks.

Father Pius sat behind his desk with his fingers pressed together. Jake ducked down out of sight, hoping that none of the cyber-monks would appear and catch him listening beneath the window.

"I am Father Pius Gates, the cyber-abbot responsible for this monastery."

"It's good to meet you, Father," said the stranger. "My name is Callidus Stone."

Jake couldn't place the accent. It seemed to

contain traces from all the languages of the seven solar systems.

"How can I help you today, Mr. Stone?"

"I'm looking for someone, a boy who came to Remota eleven years ago. A boy with a gold pendant."

Chapter 2

The Legend of Altus

"I suppose you're a relative of this boy, perhaps an uncle searching for his long-lost nephew?" said Father Pius, giving nothing away.

Jake's heart stopped while he waited for the answer.

"No, not exactly," said Callidus. "I'm what you might call a fortune seeker, someone who collects bounties and searches for lost treasure. I don't expect you to trust me, Father—we've only just met—but I can help the boy."

"Is he in trouble?"

"It's my belief that he is from Altus, and I want to take him home."

"Altus?" Father Pius sounded amused. "The mythical planet with a gold-dust desert and three crystal moons?"

"Yes, that's right."

"Why, that's nothing more than a story, an old space tale for children," said the cyber-abbot. "There's no such place."

"Just because nobody knows the location of Altus, it doesn't mean it doesn't exist."

"Many fools have wasted their lives searching for that planet."

"Do I look like a fool to you?"

"No," said Father Pius. "No, you do not. I expect you think this boy will lead you to Altus, where he'll be reunited with his people and you'll be rewarded for your trouble, perhaps with a crate of jewels. In the end, everyone will benefit and nobody will get hurt."

"Exactly."

"And what makes you believe this boy is from Altus? I mean, let's assume for a moment that both he and the planet exist, what proof do you have that he's Altian?"

"His pendant," said Callidus. "I'm not the only one searching for the boy. A group of strangers were passing through the spaceports in the seventh solar system a few weeks ago, asking questions about him. They described a gold pendant containing three precious stones: a diamond, a ruby, and an emerald. I've studied the legends and that's the symbol of Altus; each stone represents one of its crystal moons. There are also rumors of an Altian vessel being destroyed in this solar system, not far from here, but no one has ever discovered the wreckage. All the clues point to Remota, so I decided to get here first."

"Who are these people looking for the boy?" asked Father Pius, trying not to sound concerned. "What do they want with him?"

"I think that I've answered enough questions for now," said Callidus, his tone growing impatient. "It's time you gave me a straight answer, Father. Is he here?"

There was an uncomfortable silence.

"No," said Father Pius, which was true, because Jake wasn't in the monastery at that precise moment. "I'm sorry, but it would seem as though you've had a wasted journey. There are no boys here for you to help and I don't believe that Altus exists."

"I'm not someone who gives up easily, Father." Callidus sounded determined. "I'll be on Remota for a couple of weeks, should you hear anything. Please understand that the boy will be better off with me. I may not be a saint, but I'm by far the lesser evil."

The fortune seeker marched out of the office, slamming the door behind him. Jake sat with his back against the hot stone wall. Had the stranger been telling the truth about Altus?

"Jake Cutler!" A large hand grabbed hold of Jake's arm and pulled him to his feet.

"Brother Jonas!"

"What have I told you about eavesdropping on private conversations?" scolded the portly cyber-monk. "You've gone too far this time, Jake. I'm taking you to see Father Pius."

Jake sat in the cyber-abbot's office waiting for the usual lecture about behaving more responsibly. Father Pius walked around his desk to the window and glanced outside, as though trying to picture where Jake had been sitting. His expression seemed more concerned than angry.

"Did you hear everything that Mr. Stone said?"

"You mean about Altus and people looking for a boy with a gold pendant?"

"Yes." Father Pius regarded Jake with troubled eyes. "I'm not sure who they are or what they want, so until I know more, I would like you to remain in the monastery, where we can protect you."

"He was talking about me, wasn't he? Do you think Callidus Stone can take me home?" asked Jake. "Maybe he knows what happened to my dad."

"Now hold on there. Don't go getting excited," said Father Pius. "If you ask me, it sounds a little too good to be true. Isn't it every orphan's dream to discover they're from a wealthy planet?"

"I might not be an orphan. We don't know that for sure."

"My point, Jake, is that Mr. Stone isn't interested in you or your happiness. He's only after treasure."

"Are you saying he would hurt me?"

"No, I don't think so," said Father Pius. "He doesn't seem the type, but he might try to abduct you. If not him, then someone else might attempt to smuggle you off Remota."

"What are we going to do?"

"That's for me and the brothers to worry about. We always knew that someone might come looking for you one day. You'll be safe here until we can find you somewhere new to hide—perhaps a monastery in a different solar system."

Jake nodded, but his stomach tensed at the thought of people hunting for him.

"Why don't you get a bite to eat, while I talk with the brothers," said Father Pius. "How does a slice of apple pie sound?"

It sounded good. Apples were his favorite fruit and had been for as long as he could remember.

"Thanks, Father," said Jake. "If it turns out that I am from Altus, I'll pay you back for everything."

Father Pius laughed. "That's very kind, but I don't seek a reward. I look after you because I choose to, not because I have to, and because I care about you. I know that I'm not your real father, Jake, but you are like a son to me."

"Thanks, Father . . . I mean . . . you know what I mean."

Jake didn't know what else to say. He left the office, his mind still racing. Was Altus real? Would his father be waiting there? Who else was looking for him, and what would happen if they found him?

Jake had been kept inside the monastery for almost a week, under constant supervision while the cyber-monks decided where to send him. It would be strange to live somewhere other than Remota, but wasn't that what he wanted? He had always dreamed of seeing other planets, so why was he so worried?

It was driving him crazy being trapped indoors. He wasn't even allowed near the windows in case someone saw him. If that wasn't bad enough, he had been banned from sliding down the banister. During the day he only had his studies to distract him. In the evenings, he downloaded images of famous space-ships and Interstellar Navy warships to sketch for his collection. His bedroom wall was now covered in drawings, like a shrine to space travel.

The cyber-monks had taken additional security measures to protect the monastery, installing a new force field and intruder alarm. Lookouts were posted around the perimeter. No one was allowed to open the front door without at least two novices to back them up. They had programmed the house robots to guard the tech library, and Jake had heard the cyber-monks discussing the design of sonic weapons that would render people unconscious, so they could defend themselves without the need to kill. It wouldn't be the first time a religious order had taken up arms.

"Good evening," said Brother Sabir, who had come to watch over Jake in the recreation room. "Have you had a good birthday?"

"The cake was nice, but I wish I wasn't stuck indoors."

"It's not so bad in here." Brother Sabir sat down and activated his handheld computer. "I hardly ever go outside. Our research is too exciting. Just imagine unlocking the mysteries of the universe."

Sabir Khan had arrived on Remota three years ago as a novice, before working his way up to cyber-monk. He was younger than the others, but just as obsessed with computers and eager to earn his skull implants.

"All we ever do is study and worship technology," moaned Jake. "When was the last time we had some fun?"

"You must miss having friends your own age."

"I suppose." Jake had a few e-pals, but all they wanted to do was play stellar-net games. "Don't you miss your home planet?"

"Yes, of course," said Brother Sabir. "It's hard being away from my friends and family, but this is the life that I've chosen and it's important enough to make sacrifices."

"Do you ever hear from them?"

"Yes, we send each other e-comms or video messages." Brother Sabir tapped his screen and opened an image of people gathered in a garden. "This is my family back on Gazear in the fifth solar system, with their house robot, Rafiq-5."

"I wish I had a photo of my parents," said Jake.

"It must be sad not knowing them."

"*Sad?*" Jake couldn't help raising his voice. "How would you like to be dumped on a strange planet in the middle of the night, with no idea who you are or where you came from? My earliest memory is here, inside this monastery. I don't even know my parents' names. All I have is a bit of old blanket and this gold pendant."

He fetched the necklace from inside his top and held it up to the light so that the crystals sparkled.

"It's beautiful," remarked Brother Sabir.

"I take it everywhere with me, even in the shower," said Jake. "It might be valuable, but I would never sell it; not for anything."

"There are things in this universe worth more than money. You take good care of that pendant."

Jake decided to change the subject, before Brother Sabir realized it was time for bed. But as he went to speak, a huge bang shook the monastery.

"What was that?"

"I . . ." Brother Sabir looked startled as he stared at the storm hatches, but then he caught himself and rearranged his face. "I'm sure it was nothing . . . a fuel leak in the space docks or something."

There were two more blasts, followed by shouting.

"That's no fuel leak," said Jake.

Brother Jonas burst into the room, clutching a long metal lance-like device. His eyes were wide with panic.

"We're under attack," he wheezed. "Father Pius wants everyone in the tech library."

"Under attack?" said Brother Sabir. "Who is it?"

"Space pirates, a horde of bloodthirsty space pirates!"

Chapter 3

Space Pirates

More explosions rocked the monastery, causing plaster to shower from the ceiling. Brother Sabir grabbed Jake's arm and hurried into the corridor, where the other cyber-monks and novices were heading to the tech library.

They made their way to a large room with a high ceiling and no windows. It was furnished with wooden tables and workstations arranged in neat rows. The surrounding walls were loaded with computer equipment. Jake had only ever known the tech library as a tranquil place for study and research, where the cyber-monks worked in silence, but now it was a confused mass of fear and alarm.

Father Pius stood on a table and appealed for calm.

"Brothers," he said, holding up his hands. "Brothers, listen to me. The day we feared has arrived. There are more of them than we anticipated. It won't be long before they breach our defenses and enter the building."

Jake felt Brother Sabir's hand tighten around his arm. He glanced at the familiar faces of the cyber-monks and novices gathered in the room, people he had known for most of his life. A number of them held lances similar to the one carried by Brother Jonas.

"The time has come for us to unleash the power of technology," said Father Pius. "I know you're peaceful men, but we have to stand up for what is right. We must protect Jake and our monastery."

"But we don't stand a chance against the space pirates," protested one of the cyber-monks.

"I know you're scared," said Father Pius. "We knew danger was coming and we chose not to run, but to stay and fight."

A distant crash indicated that the space pirates had breached the force field. Father Pius remained on his table, waving his arms and shouting out orders, determined to make a stand despite the overwhelming odds. He dispatched the youngest cyber-monks into the corridor to face the savage horde.

"What about me?" asked Jake. "What can I do?"

Brother Sabir pulled him to the side, out of the way.

"You're very brave, Jake, but there's nothing you can do. The brothers have sworn to protect you with their lives."

Jake was horrified. "But I don't want people to die because of me."

"You're one of us," said Father Pius, climbing down from the table. "We would help any member of our order who was in danger."

"No, this is wrong." Jake shook his head in disbelief. "It has to be a mistake, I'm nobody. It can't be me they're looking for."

The sound of fighting erupted in the corridor, and Jake could hear the house robots smashing as the space pirates hurled them on to the flagstones.

"This isn't your fault, Jake," said Father Pius. "I thought we could protect you from a few intruders, but I never expected to be attacked by a whole pirate crew. All we can do is hold them off while you escape, but you must leave now."

"Leave?" Jake was confused. "How can I leave? I thought we were surrounded."

"There's another way out."

Plasma fire echoed in the corridor, followed by cries of pain.

"Go to the space docks and find a way off the planet," said Father Pius. "It's your only hope."

"Where should I go?"

"Head to the monastery on Shan-Ti, in the fourth

solar system. The cyber-abbot there, Father Benedict, will help you."

At that moment, two cyber-monks staggered back through the tech-library door, their robes charred and bloodied. One of them fired a sonic weapon back into the corridor, before collapsing onto the floor. Jake had never seen so much blood. It gushed from the cyber-monk's wounds and spread across the tiles in thick crimson pools.

None of it seemed real. It was as though he was watching a movie on the stellar-net. Jake could only imagine the horrific scenes in the corridor, as the space pirates slaughtered their way through the monastery. The stench of plasma and burned flesh drifted through the door. It was the smell of death.

The door.

Before Jake knew it, he was running across the room, pushing aside chairs and tables. He had to close the door before the space pirates reached it.

"No, Jake!" shouted Father Pius.

Jake ignored him.

"We can't hold them off," warned one of the injured cyber-monks, too weak to stand.

Jake had always been fast. He reached the entrance first and caught a glimpse of the intruders. Through the smoke and dust, a mass of dark shapes charged toward him, their silver space helmets reflecting the burning corridor, like a river of flaming skulls.

A bolt of white plasma caught the door frame next to Jake's head, scorching his hair and showering him in splinters. He slammed the door and grabbed a nearby chair to wedge under the handle. Brother Sabir dragged over a table, but it wouldn't stop the pirates for long.

"Go," shouted the cyber-monk, putting his weight behind the table and bracing for impact.

Jake ran over to Father Pius, who was crouched by a large server. Unlike the rest of the equipment in the tech library, it was as old as the monastery itself, a working antique. Father Pius leaned against its tarnished alloy casing and forced his hand through a small rubber slot. He rummaged around until he located a concealed handle. The server swung to the side to reveal a secret opening, its neglected hinges scraping against years of rust. Jake had heard rumors of secret escape tunnels, but had never managed to find one.

"Quick, into the tunnel," said Father Pius, as something heavy pounded on the tech-library door. "It will lead you down to the bottom of the hill."

Jake stepped inside and stopped.

"What about you and the others?" he asked. "Aren't you coming?"

"No," said the cyber-abbot, thrusting his hand-held computer into Jake's hand. "We'll delay the pirates for as long as we can."

"But you'll be killed."

"No arguments," said Father Pius. "Hurry now. You don't have much time."

"But—"

"Take care of yourself, Jake." Father Pius gave him a final pained look and pulled another handle.

The server slid back into place, covering the opening and plunging the tunnel into darkness. Jake stared at the sealed entrance, shocked at what was happening on the other side. It felt wrong to run away, but what other choice did he have? In a daze, he activated the computer and shone its light down the steep passageway.

"My orange blanket!" he said, patting his empty pockets.

For a brief moment, Jake considered going back to fetch the piece of cloth, before realizing how stupid that would be when the cyber-monks were dying to protect him. He didn't like leaving his precious memento behind, but an old rag was nothing when compared with the loss of innocent lives.

With a heavy heart, he started down the rough, twisting path. It wasn't easy to see where he was going and he often slipped on loose stones in his haste to escape. His hands caught on cobwebs, but he didn't mind spiders; they were like eight-legged fishermen casting their nets to catch their supper. He was more afraid of the muffled shots in the tech library behind him.

Jake kept checking over his shoulder, convinced that the pirates would find the secret opening at any moment. He was so distracted that he failed to notice the dead end until he bumped into it. His eyes studied the solid surface. Was this the bottom of the hill? How was he supposed to get out? He pushed rocks at random in the hope that one of them was a disguised lever, but nothing worked and the wall didn't look much like a door.

What if the tunnel had collapsed?

"'I must rely on technology'," he said, quoting from his studies. "Most problems can be broken down into scientific calculations."

With his back to the wall, Jake began to enter the data into the computer, but this process needed advanced logic, and he wasn't good with complex formulas. He stared blankly at the bright screen. If there was a solution, it was over his head.

"That's it," he said, holding up the device.

The answer *was* over his head. Hidden in the shadows at the top of a shaft was a small round hatch in the roof. Jake swung the light beam around and picked out a rusty ladder sticking out of the hole. Jamming the computer in his mouth, Jake grabbed the lowest rung and pulled himself up, pushing off the rocks with his feet.

The ladder was cold and slimy. Jake ignored the smell of corroding metal and climbed steadily up the narrow shaft, until he came to the hatch. He pressed his hand against the steel surface. It hadn't been opened for a long time, judging by the wad of cobwebs he wiped away.

Jake located a handle and pulled, but it refused to move. Was it locked? He tugged harder and the handle shifted a fraction, covering him in flakes of rust.

"Right," he said, his teeth still gripping the hand-held computer.

Wrapping one arm around the top rung of the ladder, Jake wrenched the handle with all his might. This time it turned and clicked into place. He used his shoulders to push open the heavy hatch and then clambered out onto a dusty floor.

Where was he?

Jake took the computer out of his mouth and scanned the surrounding walls. An assortment of crates and boxes suggested that he was in some kind of storage room. In the corner, a staircase led up to a door. He quickly replaced the steel hatch and dragged over a heavy crate to ensure it stayed shut.

"What now?" he asked himself.

Glancing around the room, he noticed a small window near the ceiling. He stacked a few crates against the wall and climbed up to the window. It was too narrow to climb through. At first all Jake could make out was acid rain falling in the night, but then he saw the bottom of Temple Hill, with its familiar crude path. He was pretty sure that he was under one of the shops or bars on the edge of the space docks, but which one?

Searching for more clues, Jake spotted something tucked behind a boulder at the bottom of the hill. Hiding in the shadows was a small space shuttle armed with a laser cannon. His eyes were drawn to the distinctive emblem on its side: a white skull in a space helmet over two crossed bones.

His heart stopped.

It was a space-pirate assault craft.

Two guards stood watch. Jake instantly recognized them as spacejackers, dressed in their scarlet combat suits with chunky space boots and silver skull-shaped space helmets. He knew their padded gloves would have special grips for scaling smooth surfaces, and their kit belts would contain useful raiding tools, such as picklocks, microdrills, and climbing ropes.

All space pirates wore helmets, which were usually shaped like scary skulls or alien heads, as well as combat suits in their crew's own colors. The combat suits were thinner than normal space suits and fitted with light armor, which meant that they were only good for short periods in space. In the stories, space-jackers personalized their outfits with patches, straps, and buckles, but not these two pirates, whose clothes looked brand new. Their weapons were not the classic laser pistol and cutlass combination either. Instead, they carried modern plasma rifles and palm grenades. It seemed that business was booming.

Jake ducked down to avoid being noticed. He had to find a way off the planet before the space pirates discovered him. With no time to lose, he climbed down the crates and headed for the door at the top of the staircase. There were voices and music on the other side, as well as a strong smell of beer and tobacco. It was most likely a bar full of mining crews on surface leave.

He wondered why the cyber-monks would have a tunnel leading to such a place when they weren't allowed to drink alcohol, but then he realized it probably hadn't always been a bar. Perhaps it had once been crew quarters or a maintenance workshop. A lot had changed over the last five years. Nobody used to go out at night before the mayor built the covered walkways on the streets.

Jake pressed his ear against the door and listened carefully, like a thief trying to crack a safe. When he was certain the coast was clear, he opened the door and slipped into the bar. It was decorated with blocks of color and lit by rows of neon lights. People were gathered around small plastic tables, clutching flasks and sharing amusing stories, while a house robot served drinks at the counter. No one seemed to be aware of the attack on the monastery, but the explosions would have been muffled by the loud music and stormy weather.

Jake shuffled along the side of the bar toward the exit. He resisted the urge to run and tried to act as though he belonged there, hoping that people were too distracted to notice him. As he reached the door, it swung open without warning and a gust of wind blew into the room. The silhouette of a man filled the doorway, his face concealed by shadows, so only his tall outline was visible against the night sky.

"Hello there," said Callidus Stone, stepping into the light. "It's a little late for a teenage boy to be in the space docks, isn't it?"

Chapter 4

The *Dark Horse*

Jake froze at the sight of the fortune seeker. He desperately tried to think of an excuse for being out at night.

"I've been . . . collecting for charity," he said. "But you're right, it's late and I must be getting back."

"Really?" Callidus spotted Jake's pendant and refused to step aside. "I'd like to make a donation, but you don't seem to have any means of collecting it."

"Ah, yes, that's because—"

"You can drop the act. I've seen what's happening on Temple Hill. I don't know how you escaped, but you can't leave this bar, not while there are space pirates outside."

Jake glanced past the fortune seeker and spotted a group of armed figures lurking in the streets.

"Get back; they mustn't see you." Callidus pushed Jake inside and closed the door. "Just stay calm and listen to me. I can help you, but you have to do as I say."

"I know who you are," said Jake. "I heard you talking with Father Pius. You're Callidus Stone, the fortune seeker."

"Yes, that's me, the one and only."

"Why should I listen to you?"

"Because you have very few options, so I suggest you come with me."

Jake hated to admit it, but the fortune seeker had a point. Callidus led Jake across the bar to a private booth at the rear. Jake recognized the man sitting at the table as the other passenger from the ship.

"Is this who I think it is?" asked the stocky man excitedly. "Wow, get a load of those purple eyes."

Callidus looked at Jake. "As we're going to be friends, why don't you tell us your name?"

"I'm Jake," he said reluctantly. "Jake Cutler."

Callidus smiled and slid into a seat. "This is my associate, Capio Craven. He's going to help us to find a ship."

"I am?" Capio slurped his drink.

"Yes, take whatever funds you need and get us three places on a vessel heading out of this solar system tonight." Callidus passed his companion a small leather coin pouch. "Start with the independent cargo haulers and avoid any commercial passenger ships. We'll wait here for you, but don't be long. We need to get out of here fast."

"No problem." Capio slipped on a suede coat. "I can't believe you did it, Cal. I can't believe you found him."

"Keep it down, you idiot. We don't want everyone to know."

Capio snatched up the coin pouch and hurried off, knocking over a stool in his haste. Callidus dimmed the table light and ordered two soft drinks. He then rested his dusty leather boots on the table and sank deeper into his chair, his eyes fixed on the door. Jake spotted a laser pistol sticking out of the fortune seeker's blue coat. He wondered what else Callidus was hiding.

"So, you reckon Altus is real," said Jake.

"Yes, that's right. I'm convinced it exists and I plan to find it with your help."

"My help? Why would I know where it is?"

"Because you're special," said Callidus. "It's my belief that you're from Altus and you hold the key to its location. You see those three precious stones embedded in your pendant?"

Jake placed a protective hand over his necklace and stuffed it back inside his top.

"According to my research, they represent the

three crystal moons of Altus, which are made entirely of precious stone: one diamond, one ruby, and one emerald. I've spent years searching for Altus. I'm positive the planet exists, and together we can prove it."

"What makes you think I'll help you?" Jake folded his arms defiantly. "I'm supposed to go to a monastery in the fourth solar system."

"I expect you want to find Altus as much as I do," said Callidus. "Besides, once we get away from the space pirates, you'll owe me a favor, and it's one that I'm anxious to collect."

"How do I know you're not working for those animals?"

"You don't, but if I was in league with them," Callidus nodded at the door, "I would have already handed you over to the pirates. Now that they know you're on Remota, we have to get you away. We need to find Altus."

Capio entered the bar as quickly as he had left, rushing over to their booth with a now empty leather coin pouch.

"Good news, Cal. I've booked us on a ship. It's an old cargo hauler called the *Dark Horse* and it departs in fifteen minutes. I spoke with the first mate and he said they could drop us at a spaceport in the next solar system. It wasn't cheap, but it's all that I could arrange at short notice."

"Great work, Capio," said Callidus. "Are the streets clear?"

"As crystal, not a space pirate in sight."

"I doubt they've gone far." Callidus stood up. "Let's make our move before they realize Jake isn't in the monastery."

Capio grabbed his bulging bag and the three of them hurried from the bar. In the street, lampposts quivered in the wind and acid rain beat on the covered walkway like a thousand snare drums. Callidus kept a hand on his laser pistol and an eye out for danger.

Jake noticed people standing at their windows and doorways, all looking in the same direction. He followed their gaze across to Temple Hill.

"No!" he cried.

To his horror, the monastery was on fire, its stone walls engulfed in flames. As he watched, the single tower collapsed in the heat, its beacon still pulsing in the night. Jake instinctively took a step toward the hill, before Callidus pulled him back.

"There's nothing you can do."

Jake knew he was right. It would be foolish to return there now. There was no sign of the space pirates, but it could easily be a trap. The cyber-monks had given their lives to save him, and Jake was determined not to waste their sacrifice.

Capio led them through the space docks, which seemed strange and daunting at night. The streets were full of creepy shadows and creaking jetties. Jake stayed close to Callidus, shivering with a mixture of cold and shock, still expecting to run into the space pirates at any moment.

The walkway seemed to go on forever before Capio stopped at a small jetty where an old cargo hauler rested in the darkness. Its silhouette looked like a stuffed bird ready for roasting, and as they got nearer Jake saw that its plump hull was coated in space barnacles and star weed. He had seen this ship before, but he had never bothered to draw such a rusting antique.

"This is the *Dark Horse*," said Capio. "I know it looks a little shabby, but I've been assured it's spaceworthy."

"*Dark Horse?*" scoffed Callidus. "More like *Fat Duck*. I suppose it will have to do."

"It's not that bad," insisted Capio, producing three passes from his coat pocket. "We've traveled on a lot worse over the years. Do you remember that long-distance freighter in the third solar system?"

"Don't remind me."

As they walked under the cargo hauler, a loading ramp lowered and two men emerged, both of whom were wearing faded green flight suits. The first was a young man with bronze skin and scruffy black hair. The other was much larger, with pale skin, grizzled hair, and huge arms. Neither of them had shaved in days.

"My name's Farid and I'm the first mate on this ship," said the younger man, collecting the passes. "This is Kodan, our master-at-arms. He's responsible for keeping the peace on board. Kodan doesn't speak much, but I wouldn't recommend upsetting him. He's not a patient man and he's been known to throw people out of air locks."

Kodan grinned, as though recalling a fond memory.

"Charming," muttered Callidus.

"The captain of the *Dark Horse* is Granny Leatherhead," said Farid. "But you won't get to meet her, because you'll be confined to your quarters for the duration of the journey. We're cargo haulers by trade, and we don't want passengers wandering about the ship. Is that clear?"

Callidus and Capio nodded in agreement, but Jake didn't like the idea of being shut away for days. Farid seemed to notice him for the first time.

"What's wrong with your eyes, boy?" he asked.

"Nothing," said Jake. "I have excellent vision."

Farid opened his mouth to say something else, but then changed his mind.

"Ahoy there, m-m-mateys," stuttered a muscular, dark-skinned man, leaning out of the cargo hold. "Hey, Farid, who are these p-p-people?"

"Passengers."

"Oh no, n-n-not again," groaned the shipmate, who had thick dreadlocks and gold teeth. "Granny Leatherhead is going to go m-m-mad. You know what she thinks about taking on p-p-passengers."

"It'll be okay. These people are paying good money," said Farid. "Now, seeing as you're here, Woorak, you can show our guests to their room on the lower deck."

The ship was no more impressive inside than it was outside. Its cargo hold was cold and damp, with poor lighting and rusting walls. The floor grating had suffered from years of wear and the air reeked of engine oil. It reminded Jake of the scrapyard at the space docks.

As they walked through a maze of aluminium containers, Jake noticed words scratched into the hold wall. He took a closer look and discovered at least fifty names carved into the rusting metal. Where had he heard of Machete Morgan and Nico Ninetails before?

Woorak led them through an open hatchway and along a narrow corridor. His footsteps were heavy, and there was something strange about the way he dragged his feet.

"Is that what happens to people who spend too much time in space?" whispered Jake.

"He's wearing gravity boots," said Callidus. "The crew have magnets attached to the soles of their feet to stop them from floating around in space. It's why the floors are metal."

Jake was surprised. "I thought that most ships used artificial-gravity systems."

"Most modern ships do, but not everyone can afford such expensive equipment."

They passed a door labeled ENGINE ROOM and stopped next to four smaller hatches.

"Here we are, valued g-g-guests," said Woorak. "These are the guest quarters. They sleep f-f-four to a room. Meals are provided three times a day, not that there's such a thing as day in space, only n-n-night, but we like to keep a routine. I suggest you get strapped in quick, because we're about to t-t-take off."

The shipmate opened one of the hatch doors and stood next to it with his hand open, as though expecting a tip. Callidus and Capio ignored him and entered the room.

"Thanks," said Jake politely, before darting through the opening behind them.

Woorak closed the hatch with a scowl and skulked back up the corridor empty-handed.

The room was exceptionally small, with copper pipes lining the ceiling. It contained two bunk beds, a tin sink, and a pull-out toilet. Acid rain lashed the porthole window, casting liquid shadows across the wall. It was like a prison cell, not somewhere you would pay to stay. Jake climbed onto one of the narrow beds and strapped himself in. The mattress was hard and the pillow stank like old socks.

As he lay there, nightmarish images of the monastery attack flashed before his eyes. He wondered if the space pirates knew he had escaped. Were they searching the space docks for him at that very moment? What if they were waiting to spacejack the cargo hauler as it left the planet?

An amber light flashed above their heads and a siren wailed. Was that a good sign? Jake hoped it was the launch signal. His heart beat faster as he listened to the loading ramp close beneath them. He felt both anxious and excited to be leaving the planet. Was the ship supposed to be making all of those noises? How safe was space travel? After all, the last time he was up there, his father's ship had crashed. He checked his straps to ensure they were fastened tight.

The engines fired up and Jake's entire body tensed. It was like caged thunder being released into the night. He gripped the mattress and braced himself. Any second now, the crew would switch the engine to full throttle and release the thrusters. Any second now, the *Dark Horse* would rise up into the sky. Any second now, Jake would head into outer space for the adventure of his life.

Chapter 5

Stir-Crazy

The exhausts of the *Dark Horse* roared like angry gods, as the old cargo hauler pulled away from the steel jetty and dragged itself into the sky. Jake was unable to move, pinned to his mattress by the force of acceleration. His whole body shook and swayed with the ship, as it was buffeted by Remota's fierce winds.

The *Dark Horse* climbed steadily through the planet's turbulent atmosphere, higher and higher, until it finally eased into the calmness of space. The exhausts fell silent, leaving only the mechanical growl of the engine. Jake shivered as the temperature dropped sharply. He then felt a strange sensation as the pressure of acceleration was replaced by weightlessness. His entire body had become as light as a feather, and only his bed straps stopped him from floating away.

Jake checked on the others. Capio had turned pale and looked as though he might throw up. He blamed it on the bumpy takeoff and refused to open his eyes. Callidus was much more relaxed. Jake couldn't help but feel thrilled to be in space; he just wished it had been for happier reasons.

Callidus released his straps and drifted from his bunk, wanting to see what was happening outside. He used his hands to move around the room, pushing himself off surfaces until he reached the porthole window. Jake waited for him to report back.

"Can you see the pirate ship?" asked Capio. "Is it a big one?"

"No pirate ships, but there is a naval warship."

"The Interstellar Navy?" Capio released his chest strap and sat up. "What are they doing here?"

"They must be hunting the space pirates," said Jake, wrestling with his own buckles.

"I've never seen a warship that size." Callidus pushed himself away from the window. "It must be some kind of super-destroyer."

"We should contact them." Jake threw off his straps and rolled into the air. "I'm sure they would protect me."

"I have a feeling that our friends aboard the *Dark Horse* would like to avoid the authorities," said Callidus, catching hold of Jake and guiding him to the porthole window. "I'm not sure what sort of cargo they're hauling, but I doubt they have a license to carry passengers."

Jake's mouth fell open at the sight of the naval warship suspended over Remota. It looked brand new and unlike anything he had ever seen in the space docks. The midnight-blue design was similar to the warships seen on the *Interstellar News*, only it was twice the size with double the laser cannon. If that ship was after the space pirates, they were in serious trouble.

The *Dark Horse* moved farther away from Remota. Jake noticed how small and gray the planet looked from space. He was leaving behind the only home he could remember. It had been his dream to escape Remota and explore the stars, but not like this, not with people dying. The thrill of the launch drained away, replaced once more by the horror of the monastery attack. Images of flaming skull-shaped helmets flared in his mind, and the screams of cyber-monks echoed in his ears. His stomach lurched at the thought of never seeing the brothers again. Never talking with them, or eating with them, or studying with them, or even being told off by them . . . ever again.

"I want to go back," he said.

"Are you mad?" Callidus hoisted himself back into his bed. "There is no going back."

"But—"

"Cal is right," said Capio. "It's no longer safe for you on Remota."

Jake watched the planet shrink into the distance, until it had completely disappeared. Whether he liked it or not, that part of his life had gone forever.

"Happy birthday," he muttered to himself.

For three days, Jake, Callidus, and Capio remained in their quarters with nothing to do except talk and watch the stars. It was like being trapped in the monastery, only with less room. The meals consisted of pots of green mush and tubes of brown paste. Jake didn't know what he was eating most of the time, but he was convinced that one breakfast was beef and custard flavor. He longed for a fresh crunchy apple.

There didn't seem much point in continuing his cyber-studies, now that the monastery had been destroyed. Instead, Jake used the handheld computer to research space pirates and Altus over the stellar-net. It made him feel as though he was doing something other than sitting around and mourning the cyber-monks. Callidus had taken a while to accept that Jake knew nothing about his home planet.

"I've read a load of articles and not one of them

proves that Altus exists," said Jake, lowering the device. "There isn't a single clue to its location, so how do we know if we're heading in the right direction?"

"We don't." Callidus was cleaning his laser pistol. "My first priority was to get you away from danger, then come up with a plan to get you home."

"Okay, we're out of danger," said Jake. "What's the plan?"

"We'll take your pendant to a crystal dealer in the next solar system and see what they can tell us."

"Is that it?" Jake was hoping for something more inspired.

"It's the only plan we have, unless you can calculate a better one on your little gadget. I had hoped you would know something about Altus."

Jake tossed the handheld computer across the room in frustration and watched it bounce off the opposite wall.

He left his bunk and drifted over to the porthole window to check out the view. It turned out that space was far less exciting than he had expected. Most of it looked the same, like a night sky passing by the ship. Capio had pointed out bright star clusters and colorful nebula clouds, but Jake had no pens and paper to draw them.

No, it wasn't much fun being shut in a small room with two adults and a single window. Jake had to get out of there or he would go stir-crazy. So what was stopping him? Okay, they weren't supposed to leave their quarters, but if he waited until the others were asleep, he could explore the ship without them ever knowing. As long as no one saw him, he couldn't get into trouble, right?

"Why are you suddenly so happy?" asked Capio suspiciously.

Jake realized that he was smiling at the idea of leaving the room.

"I saw a shooting star," he lied. "And wished for some proper food."

"If you see another one," said Capio, "order me a steak."

A few hours later, when the lights were low, Jake lay in his bunk waiting for the others to doze off. It seemed to take them forever to settle, but eventually he heard the reassuring sounds of slumber. Capio snored like a hover-bike and Callidus talked in his sleep, mumbling something about Altus.

Jake carefully released his bed straps and floated free from his bunk. After a few days in space, he had become used to moving in zero gravity and was able to maneuver himself quietly to the hatch door. Any sounds he made were disguised by the rumbling of the engine and Capio's snores.

With thief-like stealth, Jake located the control panel and pressed the release button. During the day the sound of the hatch opening was hardly noticeable; it gently slid open as the crew delivered their meals. But at night it seemed much louder, creaking and hissing like a mechanical monster. Jake winced with each noise, expecting the others to stir at any moment.

"Abandon ship!" shouted Callidus, tugging at his straps.

Jake held his breath and waited for the fortune seeker to see him, but Callidus just rolled onto his side, muttering in his sleep. With a sigh of relief, Jake pulled himself through the hatch and into the corridor, floating like a ghost in the night. The air was no fresher in the rest of the ship, but it felt good to escape from the room. He made sure there was nobody coming before gliding along the corridor, using the extra space to experiment with the zero gravity.

Was this what it felt like to fly?

"Give us a kiss," said a voice.

Jake jerked around to see who had spoken, but nobody was there. Had he imagined it? Then he noticed the engine-room door. He pressed his ear against the cold metal and listened. For a moment all he could hear was the engine thumping away in the background, before the same voice spoke again.

"Give us a kiss."

"In your dreams," said another voice.

Jake continued up the corridor. He wanted to see more of the ship and had no time to eavesdrop. Next to the cargo-hold door, a metal staircase provided access to the upper levels. Jake used his hands to climb up to a hatch on the first deck. He peered through a small window, taking care not to be seen, to find a deserted dining area lit by glowing wall panels, and beyond that, storage units and a small kitchen.

Jake's breath misted on the cold glass. He spotted some discarded food tubes and rum flasks floating in the air. His stomach rumbled at the thought of eating, but he resisted the temptation to have a midnight snack, in case someone noticed the supplies were missing. Jake continued up the levels until he reached the top deck. He knew the bridge would be located at the highest point.

Voices echoed in the darkness, leading him to an open hatch near the front of the ship. He approached the doorway with care, edging closer until he was just outside the room. His heart was beating so fast, it threatened to burst through his rib cage. There was a good chance he would be caught if he went any farther, but it would be worth it to get a glimpse of a real bridge. Unable to resist, he peeked inside.

The bridge was a circular room with a curved ceiling and low lighting. Its iron walls were covered with computer displays and star charts. The first thing Jake noticed was a wide glass window that provided a spectacular space scape. His eyes then feasted on an array of scanners and navigation equipment. He wished he could take a closer look.

Jake recognized Farid standing nearest, holding his hands behind his back. Next to him fidgeted a stout silver-haired woman, with a hooked nose and long chin, who wore a brown leather coat and chunky gravity boots. Jake guessed this was the captain of the ship, Granny Leatherhead. A young woman with dark blue hair sat at the controls, most likely the pilot. Her bucket seat was cracked and leaking stuffing. None of them noticed the thirteen-year-old boy hovering in the doorway.

"I don't like the idea of this job," croaked Granny Leatherhead. "It sounds like trouble to me."

"I'm not sure we can turn it down," said Farid. "We owe this guy a favor and he doesn't like to be disappointed. In the message he promised to make it worth our while."

"How long will it take, Nichelle?" asked Granny Leatherhead.

"A couple of days at the most," said the young woman, tying her blue hair in a tight ponytail. "I'm not happy about it either, Captain, but I agree with Farid. We don't have much choice."

Jake wondered what they were discussing and hoped it didn't mean being stuck in the guest quarters any longer than necessary. As he listened, a pile of clothes and space helmets caught his eye on a nearby shelf. There was something familiar about them, especially the silver helmets, which were shaped like skulls . . .

This was no ordinary cargo hauler. The crew of the *Dark Horse* were space pirates!

Jake gasped in surprise and immediately regretted it. He pulled himself clear of the door and scrambled back down the passage, knocking a fire extinguisher off its hook in his haste. He had to get back to the room and warn the others.

At the end of the passage, Jake threw himself down the stairwell, tumbling in slow motion until he reached the bottom. He landed with a bump and quickly righted himself. The engine-room door was visible down the corridor. Jake ignored the voices coming from the upper levels and launched his body toward the guest quarters. He slipped through the open hatch and collided with someone in the darkness.

A huge arm reached out and switched on the lights. Jake shielded his eyes and squinted at the figure in front of him. There was no mistaking that wolf-like stare. He had crashed into the one person he had most hoped to avoid: the master-at-arms, Kodan, who must have discovered the open hatch door. Jake turned in the air, attempting to swim back to the hatch, but Kodan reached out and grabbed his leg.

"Hey!" shouted Jake, unable to break the grip. "Let me go."

"What's going on?" demanded Callidus.

Capio also stirred, but Kodan simply grinned at them and tightened his hold. Granny Leatherhead stormed through the hatch, flanked by several ship-mates armed with laser pistols and cutlasses. The captain scowled at her guests with a single gray eye, the other was hidden behind a crusty leather eye patch.

Kodan held Jake up and dangled him by his leg.

"So, it was you wandering about my ship," croaked Granny Leatherhead, stomping across the room. "Wanted to take an evening stroll, did you, boy?"

"I was only looking." Jake tried to wriggle free.

"Then why did you run away? Perhaps you heard something interesting on the bridge, eh?" she said. "Maybe a dip in space will sort out your curiosity. Kodan, prepare the air lock."

"Jake?" exclaimed Callidus. "Did you leave this room?"

"Yes, but—"

"What were you thinking? We agreed to stay in our quarters until the next port."

"No wonder the crew is angry with you," said Capio, yawning.

"Angry, yes, but why are they armed?" wondered Callidus, reaching for his own pistol.

"Hands in the air, chisel chin," snapped Granny Leatherhead, pointing her gun at him.

"Do as she says," urged Jake. "This is a pirate ship."

Chapter 6

Space Dogs

Callidus raised his arms in surrender and encouraged Capio to do the same. Farid pushed past them and searched their bunks, stripping the beds and turning over the mattresses. He confiscated a laser pistol, a hunting knife, and a box of palm grenades.

"I was saving those," muttered Capio under his breath.

Granny Leatherhead caught Jake frowning at her.

"What are you gawking at, boy?"

"Are you the pirates who attacked the monastery and murdered the cyber-monks?"

"Those web-worshipping wimps?" Granny Leatherhead glared at him. "What if we were? What are you going to do about it?"

Jake let his eyes fall to the floor.

"No? I didn't think so," she said. "Well, for your information, that raid was nothing to do with us. We prefer to keep our business in the stars."

"If it wasn't you, who was it?" asked Callidus.

"We don't know." Farid shrugged. "But we figured it best to leave Remota before people started asking questions."

"We're quite famous, you know," cackled Granny Leatherhead. "We've been plundering these trade routes for twenty years, and you don't achieve that by hanging around with a hold full of stolen cargo."

Jake doubted that anyone famous would be flying around in such a rusty old ship. There were just a handful of crews who had evaded capture for that long and only one of them was led by a woman.

"That's where I've heard those names scratched on the cargo-hold wall," he said. "You're the Space Dogs."

"Well, aren't you the smart one?" Granny Leatherhead regarded him with a curious eye. "You know a bit about pirates, do you? Yes, I admit it, that's us. We're the infamous Space Dogs."

"We put the *fear* in *stratosphere*," boasted one of the shipmates.

Callidus wasn't convinced. "How do we know you weren't involved in the attack?"

"You'll just have to take our word for it," insisted Farid. "Not that you can trust a space pirate."

"I believe them," said Jake. "The clothes on the bridge were faded and black, but the pirates on Remota wore scarlet outfits."

"You see, you lily-livered losers, we're not guilty." Granny Leatherhead lowered her weapon. "But what I'm wondering is why someone would want to attack a bunch of boring cyber-skunks. Is that why you folks were in such a hurry to leave? Were they looking for you?"

"What if they were?" said Jake, unable to help himself. "What are you going to do about it?"

Granny Leatherhead raised her pistol and pointed it at his forehead.

"Don't push me, boy," she warned, prodding him with the barrel. "I'm not a nice person, so if you know something, you had better start talking. Who are you and why are you running?"

"We don't want any trouble," said Callidus. "Whatever we're paying you for this trip, I'll double it once we reach port."

The captain scratched her eye patch. "That's a tempting offer, handsome, but it won't satisfy my thirst for knowledge. Nobody's leaving this room until I get some answers. We can take your money later."

"Okay," said Callidus. "You're right. We're refugees fleeing from murderous space pirates. You saw the raiding party—they launched an unprovoked attack on us. What else can we say?"

Granny Leatherhead could tell he was withholding something.

"Talk to me, lad," she said to Jake. "I want to know who you are and what your friends are up to, or I'll get Kodan here to rip off their arms and legs."

Kodan rubbed his hands and grinned. Callidus went to protest, but Farid held a cutlass to his chest. Jake regarded the captain for a moment, wishing he could remember more about the Space Dogs. Granny Leatherhead was easily the most frightening person he had ever met and she made a lot of threats, but surely no one was cruel enough to tear off the limbs of their own passengers. It had to be a bluff.

"Do your worst," he dared her.

Granny Leatherhead stiffened, her eye twitching with anger. "Why, you cocky little . . . Fine, have it your way."

Had he guessed wrong? Kodan let go of Jake's leg and turned to the others.

"Wait, I'll talk," wailed Capio. "His name is Jake Cutler and he was raised on Remota, but Callidus reckons he's from Altus."

"Altus?" snorted Farid. "Do you take us for fools? Altus is a myth."

"Is it now?" croaked Granny Leatherhead. "I've heard of more incredible things over the years. Haven't you ever wondered where the stories come from? If there's that much smoke, maybe there's a little fire as well."

"Nice one, Capio," said Callidus through gritted teeth. "Why don't you tell them what we had for breakfast, while you're at it?"

Granny Leatherhead squared up to the fortune seeker.

"Well, big boy, how come you're so certain this planet exists? What do you know that we don't?"

Callidus considered his words carefully.

"I've only heard rumors. I was told that an Altian vessel was destroyed near Remota eleven years ago. It's my belief that Jake is one of the survivors and together we can find Altus. However, there are others searching for him."

"People who would attack a monastery?" asked Granny Leatherhead.

"Yes."

"People like you?" sneered Farid. "What wouldn't a fortune seeker do for a container full of crystals?"

Farid's words made Jake wonder if fortune seekers were any better than space pirates.

"Why does the boy need your help?" asked Granny Leatherhead.

"Nobody knows the location of Altus, not even Jake," said Callidus. "Capio and I have been researching the legends for years and we might be able to detect clues that otherwise get overlooked. It would be a mistake to think that Jake can find Altus without us."

"What about his parents? Why aren't they out looking for their little treasure?"

"His mother is dead and his father was lost in a space storm, though it's possible he survived and returned to Altus." Callidus leaned closer to the captain. "If the rumors are true, the boy is from an important family, important and wealthy, which means that there will be a reward for his safe return."

"Is that so?" Granny Leatherhead put her weapons away. "Right, wait here, you miserable moon maids, while I talk with my crew."

The space pirates left the room and closed the hatch behind them.

"Oh, that's just great," said Capio. "Do you think we'll get a last meal or will they throw us into space on an empty stomach?"

"Hey, you're the genius who booked us on a pirate ship," Callidus pointed out. "Now calm down."

"Calm down?" Capio was far from composed. "What if I don't? We're about to be killed, so there's not much you can threaten me with right now, Cal."

"Stop it," said Jake, who was glad to be back in his bunk and away from Kodan. "We need to stick together."

They were interrupted by the return of the crew, who were no longer brandishing weapons.

"Okay, gentlemen, here's the deal." Granny Leatherhead spat on her hand and held it out. "We're going to help you to locate Jake's home planet in return for half of the reward. I'm assuming our share will be enough to buy a new ship?"

"If not a small fleet of ships," said Callidus.

"Excellent." Her single gray eye sparkled with greed. "Do we have a deal?"

"Yes," said Callidus, shaking her hand. "I think we understand each other."

"As for you, my little explorer," she directed this comment to Jake. "You're going to be too busy to roam about my ship. I want you to work in the engine room for the rest of the voyage, understand?"

"Aye, Captain," he said, giving a convincing salute.

"Get some rest and then report next door to our chief engineer, Scargus. He'll tell you what to do and you must obey his every word. I expect you to work hard and I don't want any trouble, do you hear me?"

"Aye, Captain."

The crew exchanged menacing smiles and departed.

Granny Leatherhead paused by the door. "Well, what are you waiting for, boy? Get to bed. I want you in that engine room first thing."

Jake stirred the moment the lights came on and drifted from his bunk, already clothed. He rammed a food packet into his pocket and left the room, making his way down the corridor to the engine room. Worried he was late, he banged on the door with his fists. It opened to reveal a scrawny old man with a bushy gray beard who wore a string vest and crumpled cargo trousers. The man rested his thumbs inside a leather tool belt and regarded Jake through thick glasses.

"Yes?" he asked, his mouth barely visible in the forest of hair.

"Good morning, sir," said Jake politely. "My name is Jake Cutler, and I'm supposed to report to Chief Engineer Scargus so he can give me some work."

The old man laughed. "Is that what she calls me

now, her chief engineer? What a grand title for such a dirty job."

"Are you Scargus?"

"Aye, that's right. Nice to meet you, lad. Come inside."

The engine room was large and cluttered, with orange corrugated-iron walls. It was hot inside and hard to hear anything over the noise of the engine. Apart from the racket, the room felt cozy, with low lighting and music. There was even a collapsed sofa bolted to the floor and a hammock billowing between two pillars. Diagrams and blueprints plastered the walls, along with a variety of tools that were trying to escape their hooks.

Scargus closed the door and patted Jake on the back, sending him spinning across the room. A young woman in grease-stained overalls appeared from behind the engine, holding a wrench. Her other arm looked artificial.

"Hello," she said, wiping oil from her cheek. "We don't get many passengers in here. I'm Manik, Manik the mechanic. I help Scargus keep this old tub spaceworthy."

Manik had short dirty-blonde hair and could have easily passed for a boy. Jake recognized her voice from earlier, but who had asked her for a kiss?

"Fart face, dog breath, grubby guts," screeched a voice behind him.

Jake turned in surprise to discover a large parrot clinging to a perch.

"This is Squawk." Manik walked over to the bird. "He's a funny old beast, what you might call temperamental."

"Aye, *temper* and *mental* are the two words I would use to describe him," said Scargus.

"He's not that bad." Manik scooped a handful of bird feed from her pocket. "I like talking to him when I'm down here on my own, but then again, I'm always talking. Scargus says it's because I'm hyperactive, which is funny, because my name sounds like manic, which means . . . Oh, there I go again, talking too much."

"I've never met a real parrot," said Jake. "Does he bite?"

"Only if you forget to feed him." Manik held up her artificial hand.

"Squawk did that?"

"No, only kidding," she said. "I lost my arm to a faulty engine on a passenger ship. It was an accident, but they still blamed me for stranding two hundred commuters in the fourth solar system. Nobody would employ me after that, until I met Scargus. He helped me rig up this fake limb."

Manik wiggled her robotic fingers, which looked as though they belonged to a clumsy metal skeleton.

"Give us a kiss," screeched Squawk, flapping his wings and sending feathers spiralling into the air.

"Silence, you overgrown canary!" barked Scargus. "Manik, young Jake is going to be assisting us for the next few days. Why don't you show him around and explain how everything works? Just don't forget to breathe between sentences."

"Sure thing," she replied, putting away her wrench. "Come on, Jake, let me show you what's keeping this heap of space junk moving."

Manik spent the next few hours introducing Jake to the ship's engine, explaining in great detail how it turned fuel cells into thrust, which propelled the vessel through space. The engineer's mate was enthusiastic about her subject and used lots of technical terms. Jake found it difficult to keep up. He kept smiling and nodding to avoid hurting her feelings.

"Is there any way to make it quieter?" he asked.

"No, not without replacing the whole thing," she said. "It would be cheaper to buy a new ship and that's not going to happen any time soon."

"How come you don't have an artificial-gravity system?"

"We do." She pointed at a large metal cylinder in the corner of the room. "It was installed a couple of years ago, but Granny Leatherhead says it uses too much energy, so she's banned us from using it. I'm sure we could turn it on in an emergency. Until then we're stuck with our gravity boots."

"I wish I had some." Jake was struggling to keep still. "Do you have any I can borrow?"

"I doubt we have your size—we don't usually allow children on the ship—but there might be something I can do for you."

Manik opened a storage compartment and rummaged inside.

"Here we go," she said, holding up a couple of metal strips and some wire. "We can tie these magnets to the soles of your shoes. They won't be as effective as gravity boots, but they should help you stay on the ground."

Jake tried out his makeshift gravity shoes, walking across the engine-room floor. He found it difficult to lift his feet, because the magnets were so powerful, but it was still less effort than floating around the ship.

"Thank you," he said. "I thought pirates were supposed to be mean and tough, but you're both, well, really nice."

Manik laughed. "Did you hear that, Scargus?"

"It sounds as though you've been reading too many stories, eh lad?" Scargus had been watching Jake take his first space steps. "I'll tell you what, now that you can walk, why don't you stroll over to the other side of the room and make us all a pot of tea, and then I'll teach you some real pirate history."

Chapter 7

Zerost

The next two days aboard the *Dark Horse* went by surprisingly fast. Jake spent most of his time in the engine room doing odd jobs. He also made copious amounts of "pirate tea," brewed using two tea bags, three sugars, and powdered milk, in a gravity-proof pot. In return, Scargus and Manik taught him space shanties and told him stories from pirate history.

"My ancestors were famous sea pirates of old," said Scargus, sipping his tea. "They sailed the great Kayef oceans in search of merchant ships to plunder, until they were caught and hanged for their crimes."

"Who were the first space pirates?" asked Jake.

"According to legend, the first spacejackers had once been peaceful colonists. They settled on the ice planet Zerost, in the fifth solar system, until one day they lost contact with their sponsor, the Galactic Trade Corporation, whom they relied on for food and medical supplies."

"I've heard of them," said Jake. "Their drills are all over Remota."

He knew the Galactic Trade Corporation was the number one crystal supplier in the galaxy. Most independent colonies had their own currency, such as the Remota pound or Reus dollar, but crystals were accepted everywhere.

"At the time, the Galactic Trade Corporation was only a small company struggling to survive a mega-depression," explained Scargus. "When the directors realized the only gems on Zerost were ice crystals, they abandoned the planet and left the colonists to fend for themselves."

"What happened?"

"In desperation, the colonists took to the stars in their shuttle craft, but they were so far from the nearest spaceports, they were forced to steal from passing ships."

"And most vessels don't give up their precious provisions without a fight." Manik was finding it hard not to talk. "The colonists had to become space pirates to survive."

"After the mega-depression, things started to improve," continued Scargus. "The Galactic Trade Corporation grew wealthier and more powerful, despite claims that they mistreated their miners."

"But that's not fair," said Jake.

"It makes you wonder who the real criminals are, doesn't it?"

"What happened to the colonists?"

"Well, they continued to spacejack passing vessels until the Interstellar Government sent a fleet of naval warships to Zerost." Scargus scrunched up his face with bitterness. "The space pirates were off-world that day, but it didn't stop the Interstellar Navy from destroying their homes and killing their families."

"That's awful," exclaimed Jake. "I had no idea the Interstellar Navy was so ruthless. They're supposed to be the good guys."

"It's not something the United Worlds put in their storybooks," said Scargus. "The space pirates were forced to abandon Zerost and travel the seven solar systems in stolen ships. Many modern space-jackers can be traced back to those colonists from Zerost."

"Does that include you?"

"No, most of the Space Dogs are just your average criminals, recruited from illegal spaceports or freed from prison ships," said Scargus. "Granny Leatherhead, on the other hand, is a direct descendant. That woman was born on a pirate ship and she'll probably die on one. It's in her blood, the family trade. Few people despise the Galactic Trade Corporation more than old Lizzy."

"Lizzy?"

"Elizabeth Leatherhead," said Manik. "That's her real name."

It was strange hearing Granny Leatherhead referred to as anything other than the captain.

"So why do people let the Galactic Trade Corporation get away with it?" asked Jake. "Why doesn't the Interstellar Government do something?"

"Money," said Scargus. "It's no longer about survival of the fittest, but survival of the richest. I expect that half of the Interstellar Government has been bribed at some point."

"Is that why you became a pirate, so you can make a fortune?"

"Ha, shiver my circuits, lad. I've been on this ship for twenty years and we barely steal enough to feed ourselves. It's the reason the captain wears an eye patch, because she can't afford a replacement eye, or so she tells us. Life as a space pirate is mostly hard work and hiding from the Interstellar Navy."

"But what about all those containers in the cargo hold?"

"Empty, most of them."

"Maybe you should try being full-time cargo haulers," suggested Jake.

"Go legitimate?" Scargus almost choked. "It's too late for this crew to earn an honest living, Jakey-boy. Besides, we still hope to find the big one, the elusive treasure that will make us rich beyond our dreams. It's out there somewhere, waiting for us in the big black. I just hope we discover it before it's too late."

"Too late?"

"Not every buccaneer makes it to retirement," said Scargus. "Apart from Granny Leatherhead, I've been here the longest."

"I bet you were a great pirate." Jake tried to picture the old engineer as a younger man.

"Aye, not bad," said Scargus, fetching his faded black pirate outfit from a dented locker. "Here, take a look at this, it's my old space helmet and combat suit. I've worn them on more than a hundred jobs over the years. Each patch represents a victory. This blue one is for the great Reus Heist, and that round one is for the Service Port Raids."

"You were part of the Service Port Raids?" Jake almost let go of his cup with excitement. "Is it true you actually spacejacked a whole service port? How do you make something like that disappear?"

"Ha, it didn't really disappear," said Scargus. "We towed it away and sold it to the space mafia to use as an illegal spaceport. Nobody would recognize it today."

Jake pointed to a cutlass mounted on the wall.

"Is that your sword?"

"Aye, that it is." Scargus unclipped the weapon and passed it down. "I once carried this everywhere, but I've not used it in years."

Jake took the sword and held it in the air. It was the first time he had wielded a cutlass, or any other weapon for that matter, and he was surprised at how light it felt in zero gravity. Unable to resist the urge, he swung it back and forth.

"It's magnifty," he said, handing the cutlass back.

Scargus put his hands in his pockets. "Perhaps you should keep hold of it for a while. You look as though you could do with the practice."

"Really?" Jake was thrilled. "Thanks, Scargus. Will you teach me how to fight?"

Scargus ignored the snickers coming from Manik. "Why not? It would be my pleasure, lad."

In the evening, Jake returned to his quarters to eat and sleep. The others were still confined to the room and they were eager to hear his news.

"Father Pius would never have let me use a sword," said Jake. "He would have told me to have faith in technology, because violence is not the answer."

"It depends on the question," argued Callidus. "You have to stand up for yourself and that takes more than a pocket full of microchips. The cyber-monks tried to defend themselves on Remota, didn't they?"

"That was different. They were attacked," said Jake. "Surrender wasn't an option. They had to use technology to protect themselves."

"Exactly, you never know when you'll need to fight." Callidus smiled. "If you want, I can continue your training once we make port in the next solar system."

"Thanks, Cal, but I don't think we're going there now." Jake squeezed the last bit of food from his packet. "I heard Scargus tell Manik that we're changing direction to a spaceport in this solar system."

"What!" exclaimed Capio.

"Which port?" asked Callidus. "Did they mention its name?"

"I'm not sure," said Jake, worried that he'd got it wrong. "They said something about picking up special cargo in Poppadoms."

"Poppadoms?" Capio looked at the tub of yellow mush in his hand. "I've never heard of a spaceport being named after food. Do you think they sell a lot of curry there?"

"It's not 'poppadoms,' you fool," said Callidus. "It's Papa Don's, an illegal spaceport owned by the space mafia."

Jake had never heard of Papa Don's, but it didn't sound friendly. "What happens in an illegal spaceport?"

"It's the sort of place you only visit if you're doing something dishonest," said Callidus. "The space mafia provides protection in exchange for a hefty docking fee."

"Why would we be heading there?" wondered Jake. "What did they mean by picking up special cargo?"

"I don't know, but at least they didn't say they were dropping off passengers." Callidus glanced out of the porthole window. "Whatever the reason, we'll find out soon enough, because we're less than a day away."

"How do you know?" asked Jake. "Have you been there in the past?"

"I don't have a past," said Callidus. "At least not one that I care to remember."

The hatch slid open and Woorak entered.

"Hello, valued g-g-guests. Have you f-f-finished eating?"

"Never mind that," said Callidus. "Why are we heading to Papa Don's? We agreed to set course for the next solar system."

"H-h-hey, take it easy, pal. We're just taking a little d-d-detour, that's all."

"A detour?" scoffed Capio.

"Y-yes, we were contacted by the m-m-man himself," said Woorak. "Papa Don wants us to do a job for him."

"What kind of job?" demanded Callidus.

"Seriously, calm down. It's not a big d-d-deal." Woorak held up his hands. "All we have to do is p-p-pick up a package for delivery. It's what we do here on the *Dark Horse*. We haul c-c-cargo."

"How long will it take?" asked Jake. "What's in the package?"

"Sorry, little fella, I've told you e-e-everything I know. If you have any m-m-more questions, I suggest you ask Granny Leatherhead."

Woorak grabbed a handful of empty food packets out of the air and left the room before anyone could ask him another question. Was he telling the truth? Whatever the reason for the change in direction, they were going to Papa Don's spaceport, whether they liked it or not.

*　　*　　*

After twelve painfully slow hours, Jake spotted something out of the porthole window. In the distance, near the Tego Nebula, there was a large metallic object rotating in space, with the name *Papa Don's* painted on its hull. It was almost as big as the naval warship they had seen over Remota, though not as well armed. Three small ships orbited the spaceport, like horses on a carousel, awaiting permission to dock.

"The space mafia set up the port next to the Tego Nebula for protection," said Callidus. "Most nebulae are just giant clouds of space dust, but this one is special. It's ionized with electricity, which helps to shield Papa Don's from attacks."

"How come?" asked Jake.

"Because the static interferes with a spaceship's computers and weapon systems, making them unreliable. It means the spaceport has difficulty with its own technology, but that's a small price to pay for free natural defenses."

"Won't the *Dark Horse* be affected?"

"Yes," said Callidus. "The pilot will have to steer the ship in manually. We had better strap ourselves in."

It wasn't the first time the Space Dogs had visited Papa Don's, and the landing was surprisingly smooth, with only a few bumps and scrapes along the way.

The *Dark Horse* pulled up alongside a docking bay in the spaceport. Jake couldn't see much through the porthole window, only dark metal walls and thick rubber pipes. The sound of industrial machinery and loud voices could be heard outside. A few minutes later, the hatch to their room opened and Granny Leatherhead stomped in with Farid and Kodan.

"Okay, listen up, you gutless guffoons," she croaked. "We're stopping here to refuel and pick up cargo. I know you've been stuck in this room for five long days, so I'm going to let you stretch your legs. I know, I know, I'm too kind, but don't go getting any ideas about running off, because if you try anything funny . . ."

Granny Leatherhead nodded to Kodan, who pulled a finger across his throat.

"Thanks for the offer," said Callidus. "But if it's all the same with you, we'd rather stay here, away from the galaxy's most-wanted criminals."

"I'm sorry, mister fortune stinker, but you don't have any choice in the matter. I want you off my ship for a couple of hours. Farid and Kodan will keep you out of trouble."

Granny Leatherhead turned and left the room.

"Come on," said Farid, standing by the door and clapping his hands. "Let's get moving."

Chapter 8

Papa Don's

Jake shivered as he walked down the loading ramp and stepped onto the docking bay, which was one of a hundred surrounding the main service hub. The spaceport was bitterly cold and it reeked of fuel, but at least there was oxygen and artificial gravity. Around him, rust-colored condensation trickled down the walls, as though the spaceport itself was bleeding. Jake had never seen such an incredible structure—a whole city in space.

As the others joined him, he noticed a number of cargo haulers docked in the neighboring bays, most of them old and damaged. He wondered if they were also pirate ships in disguise, either there on business or hiding from the Interstellar Navy.

"Hey, I know that vessel," he said, pointing to a large black cruiser laden with laser cannon. "That's James Hawker's ship, the *Lost Soul*. It's the most wanted spacecraft in the galaxy."

"Keep your voice down," hissed Farid. "And stop

pointing. We don't want any trouble, especially not with him."

Farid was right to be cautious of such a feared and famous pirate. Jake suddenly felt exposed and moved closer to Callidus.

"Do you think it's safe here?" he whispered.

"Not in the slightest," said the fortune seeker. "Just stay close to me and don't do anything stupid."

Farid led them across a floating pontoon to the main service hub, while Kodan followed behind to make sure nobody strayed. Jake wasn't used to gravity after days in space, and he found it difficult to walk without dragging his feet. He wished he had removed the magnets from his shoes.

"Where are we going?" he asked.

"For a stroll," said Farid. "If you're lucky, we'll stop for a bite to eat on the way."

"Will we pass a crystal dealer?" asked Callidus.

"That can be arranged." Farid waved his identification card at a wall scanner. "I know some people who specialize in stolen jewels. Are you buying or selling?"

"Neither, I just need some information to help us find Altus."

The entrance door slid open, releasing a medley

of music and voices, mashed with the clatter of tools and machinery.

Capio held his nose. "What's that smell?"

"Welcome to Papa Don's," said Farid, wafting the air. "You'll get used to the stench of recycled oxygen and faulty sewage systems . . . after a while."

Jake had expected the criminal underworld to be dark and scary, but the main hub was bustling with colorful characters. He had never seen so many tattoos and piercings, or such a variety of clothes and hairstyles. There were even luminous hair dyes and spray tans that glowed in the shadows. It was like being at a space carnival.

A number of people had robotic limbs and implants. Jake guessed they must be tough veterans who had seen action in many space battles. This made him feel small and intimidated, so it was reassuring to pass two security guards in riot gear. The men carried old-fashioned machine guns and combat knives, with two-way radios clipped to their belts. It appeared that even illegal spaceports needed some level of law and order.

Kodan nodded to the guards, who bobbed their heads in reply. One of them glanced at Jake, perhaps surprised to see a teenage boy. As their eyes met, something strange happened to Jake's vision, causing him to stop and hold on to the wall.

"Are you okay?" whispered Callidus.

The guards slowed down, their hands resting on their machine guns.

"It's my eye implants," said Jake. "There's something wrong with them. My sight is scrambled."

What was going on? All he could see were rough shapes swimming in a sea of static.

"Here, take my arm. We have to keep walking."

Callidus led Jake up the corridor to a quieter section, away from the guards.

"That's better," said Jake, his vision clearing. "It was horrible, like I was going blind or something."

"Has that ever happened before?"

"No, never."

"Perhaps it was the nebula," suggested Farid.

"Yeah, maybe," said Jake. "But then why has it stopped?"

Nobody knew the answer. What he needed was a cyber-monk, but there wasn't likely to be one in Papa Don's. Jake rested until he was sure his eyes were okay, and then continued up the corridor.

Inside the spaceport were ten main halls connected by long walkways. These were lined with shops and market stalls, where you could purchase everything from rare animals to illegal weapons. Jake spotted one stand advertising fake United Worlds passports and another selling stolen hover-bikes. There was even a one-armed house robot hawking hacker software. Farid and Kodan had to push away the more persistent traders.

As they passed a rough-looking bar, Jake heard a loud commotion inside. He peered through the door and saw a massive brawl taking place. At least thirty shipmates were trading punches and kicks, while others launched themselves off tables onto unsuspecting targets. Two men spilled out onto the walkway next to him, exchanging blows. As far as Jake could determine from their tattoos, it was a fight between two crews: the Starbucklers and the Crimson Hulls.

"Watch out!" warned Capio.

Jake ducked as a bar stool flew out of the door, missing him by inches.

"Come on," said Callidus, pulling him clear. "We've got a crystal dealer to find."

The five of them walked on through the port for an hour before they came to a row of shops set behind barred windows. Jake could see displays of jewelry and antiques for sale, most likely stolen goods. Farid pointed to a cracked glass door.

"ANNIE TEAK's," said Callidus, reading the sign above the window.

"I know it doesn't look like much," conceded Farid. "But she knows her stuff. Annie used to work in a crystal museum in the first solar system, before she got caught stealing. Just don't tell her I'm here, because I owe her money."

Callidus took Jake inside the narrow shop, while the others waited on the walkway. The walls were covered with valuables, ranging from gold-plated pistols to ancient wrist computers. Annie was a middle-aged woman with cropped yellow hair, sitting behind the counter reading an old paperback novel.

"Excuse me," said Callidus. "I wonder if you could take a look at something for us."

Jake pulled out his pendant.

"Is that gold?" she asked, squinting.

"Yes," said Jake.

"I'll give you ten Reus dollars for it."

Jake tightened his grip. "It's not for sale."

"Okay, twenty, but that's my final offer."

"That's not why we're here," said Callidus. "We were hoping you could tell us something about the pendant."

Annie put her book down and prodded the three crystals.

"It looks old, really old," she said. "I don't recognize the design. It's possibly from the fifth solar system, but the gold is definitely local—that greenish tint is unique to the seventh solar system. I've never seen such colorful crystals. Where did you get it, boy?"

"My dad gave it to me."

"A likely story. Are you sure you don't want to sell it?"

"Positive." Jake slipped the pendant back inside his top.

"Well, let me know if you change your mind." Annie picked up her novel and started to read again.

Jake didn't move. There was one more question he wanted to ask. "Could it be from Altus?"

Annie glared at him over her book. "Is that supposed to be funny, boy? I don't have time for jokes. Take your humor elsewhere, before I call security."

"But—"

Callidus grabbed Jake's arm and pulled him outside, where the others were waiting.

"Did you get the information you wanted?" asked Farid.

"Not exactly," said Callidus.

Jake shook off the fortune seeker's grip. "That was our best clue. How will we find Altus now?"

Callidus didn't respond.

"Cal will think of something," said Capio confidently. "He always does."

"He'd better," warned Farid. "Granny Leatherhead doesn't like bad news. Let's get some food and head back to the ship."

It was several hours since they had last eaten. Farid knew a place nearby that sold stellar-burgers, made from real meat farmed there in the spaceport. Jake didn't dare ask what kind of animal.

The café was just a small cabin with a few cheap tables scattered out front, but after five days of nothing except liquid meals, the sensation of eating solid food was amazing. Farid even managed to rustle up some applesauce for Jake, which he spread generously over his burger.

"Thanks, Farid. You know what? I don't reckon space pirates are as bad as everyone makes out."

"We're not all that good either," laughed the first mate, munching his burger.

"SECURITY TO BAY SEVEN. SECURITY TO BAY SEVEN," boomed a loudspeaker above them. "THIS IS AN EMERGENCY. RIOT IN PROGRESS."

"I don't like the sound of that," said Callidus. "Where's bay seven?"

"Not far from here," said the first mate.

"Which bay are we docked in?" asked Capio, wiping his mouth.

"Fifty-three, which is miles away," said Farid.

In the distance came the sound of shouting and banging. A team of security guards rushed by the café and disappeared down the walkway. As they passed, Jake felt his vision flicker. What was wrong with him?

"SECURITY TO BAY SEVEN. SECURITY TO BAY SEVEN," repeated the speaker. "THIS IS AN EMERGENCY. RIOT IN PROGRESS."

"Come on," said Callidus, standing up. "Let's get away from here."

The disturbance grew louder and more security guards appeared, weapons at the ready. A nearby window blew out, and a cloud of stun gas exploded.

"Too late," shouted Capio. "Here they come."

The guards retreated back up the walkway, pursued by a mob of angry space pirates in khaki combat suits. They were chanting abusively and throwing bottles. Farid shoved aside tables to create a path back to the walkway, but they were caught between the security guards and the space pirates. As Jake crouched to avoid the stun gas, his eyes flooded with static.

"Help, I can't see," he said, but his voice was lost in the uproar.

The walkway filled with smoke, and fighting broke out. In the confusion, Jake felt his way through the crowd, squeezing between heavy bodies, occasionally catching a fist or elbow. He pushed his way clear and staggered into open space, his hands held out in front of him. Where was he? What was wrong with his eyes? Were the others okay?

As Jake moved away from the riot, his vision improved. He wiped the smoke from his eyes and spotted Callidus trying to break through a wall of security guards.

"Let me pass," demanded the fortune seeker. "I'm not a rioter."

Next to him, Capio was being restrained by two guards, but Farid refused to cooperate and it took four guards to hold Kodan.

"Hey," cried Jake. "Leave them alone."

Two of the security guards broke away and lunged at Jake through the smoke, their arms outstretched. His vision scrambled, but he instinctively ducked their fat fingers and rolled to the side, narrowly avoiding the edge of the walkway.

"Run, Jake!" shouted Farid. "Get back to the ship and tell the captain what has happened."

Jake leaped to his feet and ran up the walkway, barely able to see where he was going. The two guards lumbered after him, like a couple of over-weight bears.

"Stop!" shouted one of them.

Jake cursed the magnets on his shoes for slowing him down. He threw random objects onto the metal floor behind him, forcing the guards through an obstacle course of tables, chairs, and trash cans. The traders cheered at the free entertainment.

Jake ran for what seemed like hours, chasing along walkway after walkway. He was half-blind, his feet hurt, and he had a cramp. If only he could stop for a moment to rest.

Just as he thought his lungs might burst, he heard a small explosion up ahead. He searched for the source of the noise, fearing another riot. Two red-faced men were sprinting toward him, pursued by a hobbling security guard.

"Clear the walkway," cried the men.

"Stop them," shouted the guard.

Jake threw himself into a doorway and watched the two men pass. It was only then that he noticed they were chained together. He poked his head back out and saw them charge straight into the two guards who were chasing him. Seizing his opportunity to escape, Jake slipped away while the three security guards restrained the red-faced men.

When he reached the next walkway, he realized that he was alone in an illegal spaceport, surrounded by space pirates, and he had no idea where he was going. This section was different from the rest. There were no docking bays or traders, only rows of iron doors with barred windows. It meant that he had either found a very secure hotel or he had stumbled into the prison block.

Jake spotted a large hole in the wall where there should have been a cell. Its charred edges were still smoking, and a mangled iron door swung on its remaining hinge. He wondered if the riot had just been a diversion so the two men could escape.

"Hello?" he called, to see if the coast was clear.

Jake passed an abandoned reception desk and felt his vision worsen. A two-way radio hummed and crackled in its charger. He picked it up and held it close to his head, causing the static to dance wildly in front of his eyes.

That was it!

Most modern communicators relied on the stellar-net, but the security guards in Papa Don's were forced to use older technology, because of the nebula cloud. It had to be the radio waves interfering with his eye implants. He switched off the device and his sight was restored instantly.

Jake ventured farther inside the prison block, hoping to find another exit. He resisted the urge to peek through the cell windows, deciding that only the most despicable criminals would be imprisoned in an illegal spaceport. As he passed door after door, his ears picked up a mixture of coughs, grunts, and snores.

At the end of the row, Jake stopped. There was a new sound that stood out from the others, a sound that didn't belong there. Was that singing? He pressed his ear against the last cell door and listened. Yes, there was definitely someone singing on the other side, with possibly the most beautiful voice he had ever heard.

Chapter 9

The Crystal Hunters

Jake glanced cautiously through the small barred window in the door, ready to duck if the singer turned out to be a crazed inmate. The cell was a gloomy metal box decorated with graffiti, not much bigger than his room in the monastery. A young girl sat on the floor with her head in her hands. He couldn't see her face, only the long black hair resting on her shoulders. Her cream tunic and denim leggings were dirty and worn but looked as though they had once been expensive, as did her scuffed ankle boots.

"Hello," he whispered.

"Huh?" she looked up to see who had spoken. "Who's there?"

"Up here," he said, holding on to the window bars. "I'm Jake Cutler. What's your name?"

"Kella," she sniffed. Her emerald-green eyes reminded him of polished apples. "Kella Anderson. What are you doing here? Are you a prisoner as well?"

"Me? No, I've lost my way," he said, a little embarrassed.

"Where are the guards?" she asked. "I heard an explosion."

"There was a breakout. The guards will be back soon."

Jake checked the corridor, listening for footsteps. Kella stood up and approached the door, her eyes wide and desperate.

"Can you let me out?" she whispered.

"What?"

"Can you open the door, before the guards return?"

"I don't have a key," he said, tugging at the bars. "Are you okay?"

"Not really."

"No, I guess not." Jake glanced around the cell. "This is the last place I would expect to find someone singing."

"Oh, you heard that?" Her cheeks blushed. "I like the way my voice echoes in this room," she said modestly.

"It sounded pretty good out here as well."

"Do you have any food on you?" Kella wiped her tiny nose with her sleeve. "I'm so hungry and the meals here are awful."

"No, sorry, I just had a burger."

"Lucky you," she said sarcastically. "I'll remember that while I'm eating my slop."

"Hey, take it easy. You're not the only one with problems."

Kella eyed him curiously. "Are you one of those independent colonists?"

"What's that supposed to mean?" Jake didn't like the tone of her voice. "I expect you're from one of those stuck-up United Worlds."

"How dare you?" she said. "Do I look stuck-up?"

"No, but you don't look like a criminal either."

"That's because I'm not a criminal."

"So how come you're a prisoner? What did you do?"

"I didn't do anything," she huffed. "I'm innocent."

"What, they locked you up for no reason?"

"Yes." Kella folded her arms and turned her back to the door. "If you're not going to help me, you might as well get lost."

"I am lost."

"Go away and leave me alone."

"No need to be so bossy," he yelled. "It's not my fault you got caught."

Jake hadn't meant to shout. He just wasn't used

102

to being around other teenagers, especially not grumpy girls. He knew he should apologize, but as he began to speak, a large hand grabbed his shoulder and pulled him away from the door.

"What are you doing here, imp?" demanded a thin, rat-faced man who wore a black fur coat and had claw marks tattooed across both cheeks.

Behind him stood a bald woman in a pink body-suit. Her painted fingernails looked like colorful claws.

"Nothing," claimed Jake. "I'm not doing anything, honest."

"We don't see many children in Papa Don's," said the woman. "Do we, Kain?"

"No, Jala, we don't."

"I'm on my way to bay fifty-three," said Jake. "My friends are waiting there."

"Is that so?" Kain noticed the gold chain around Jake's neck. "What do we have here?"

Jake tried to resist as the rat-faced man pulled out his pendant, but he stopped struggling when Jala flashed a sharp-looking dagger. Kain seemed intrigued as he turned the pendant in his fingers. The crystals seemed to sparkle more brightly in the dimly lit walkway.

"Hello there, my beauty," said Kain, his mouth curling into a sinister smile.

"Are you space pirates?" asked Jake.

Jala laughed unkindly. "No, we're crystal hunters."

"How do you hunt crystals? I thought you had to mine them out of the ground."

"Mine crystals? Us?" she scoffed. "We acquire rare jewels and sell them to the space mafia for a fraction of the price charged by the Galactic Trade Corporation."

"'Acquire'?" said Jake. "You mean *steal* them."

"Watch your tongue, or we'll cut it off," warned Kain. "Where did you get this pendant?"

"It belongs to me."

"What is it, Kain?" asked Jala.

"If I'm not mistaken, this pendant is from Altus."

"Altus?"

Kain nodded.

"Are you sure?"

"I know quality when I see it." Kain turned to Jake. "Am I right?"

Jake swallowed hard.

"It's just a cheap souvenir," he lied, "from one of the trader's stalls."

Kain studied Jake's face and then sniffed him, as though trying to detect fear.

"You're lying to me," he hissed, grabbing Jake by

the throat. "You had better start telling the truth or I'll rearrange your pretty-boy face."

"Easy, Kain," said Jala. "He's just a kid."

"So what? He's old enough to be wandering around an illegal spaceport on his own, isn't he?" Kain leered at Jake. "What's it going to be, imp?"

For a brief moment, Jake considered telling the crystal hunters everything, but then a familiar voice interrupted them.

"Jake Cutler, what are you doing here?"

Granny Leatherhead stomped toward them, accompanied by one of her crew and two of Papa Don's security guards. Jake's eyes immediately started to flicker.

Kain let go of the pendant. "You know this space urchin?"

Granny Leatherhead planted her hands on her hips. "Aye, he's my cabin boy and he's in big trouble. Thank you for finding him, but I'll take it from here. Don't let me stop you from going about your business."

Kain's face reddened, but Granny Leatherhead held his stare without flinching. The two security guards cocked their weapons deliberately.

"You're too kind," said Kain through gritted teeth, before storming off down the walkway with Jala.

Granny Leatherhead made sure they were gone before turning to Jake, her hands still resting on her hips.

"I can explain," said Jake. "There was a riot near bay seven and the others were arrested. I was supposed to return to the ship to get help, but I lost my way."

Granny Leatherhead rolled her good eye to the ceiling.

"Do you attract trouble everywhere you go?" she asked. "Listen up, you mischief maker, Maaka here will take you back to the *Dark Horse*, while I sort out this mess."

Maaka Metal Head was a gnarly-looking ship-mate with a face full of piercings. His numerous scars suggested that he was an experienced fighter.

"Can't we stick together?" asked Jake, hoping to speak with Kella again. "What if the crystal hunters come back?"

"Ha, those blithering buffoons?" screeched Granny Leatherhead. "I'd like to see them try. Don't worry about me, short stuff. You get back to the ship. I still have some cargo to collect."

"But what about the cells? There's a girl—"

"I don't want to hear it," snapped Granny Leatherhead, her patience running out. "There's

106

nothing here that concerns you. Now get back to the ship, before I lose my sense of humor."

Jake knew it was useless trying to argue. He let Maaka lead him back to the *Dark Horse* bay fifty-three. Nichelle and Woorak were waiting in the cargo hold.

"What happened?" asked Nichelle, brandishing a hot pot of tea. "Where are the others?"

"It's okay," Maaka assured her. "There was a mix-up with security, but the captain's dealing with it."

Nichelle groaned. It probably wasn't the first time members of the crew had been arrested in a spaceport.

"You'd better get to the engine room, Jake," she said, putting down the pot and tying back her blue hair. "Tell Scargus and Manik to prepare for a quick getaway."

It was over an hour before Granny Leatherhead returned to bay fifty-three with the others. Farid and Kodan seemed in a particularly foul mood as they boarded the *Dark Horse*, closely followed by Callidus and Capio. Behind them, Granny Leatherhead and the security guards wheeled a coffin-shaped crate onto the ship.

Once they were back in the guest quarters, Capio

told Jake about the ordeal. "We were left in a holding cell with four drunken pirates who insisted on singing space shanties. It was the longest two hours of my life."

"How did Granny Leatherhead get you out?" asked Jake.

"I'm not sure," said Capio. "I expect she explained how it was all a misunderstanding."

"Perhaps." Callidus sounded doubtful. "But why would she stick her neck out for us? After all, she already had you, Jake, so she could have grabbed Farid and Kodan and left Capio and me to rot."

"Maybe she likes you," said Jake.

"No, she must need us for something."

"You told her that I wouldn't be able to find Altus without your knowledge," said Jake. "I bet that's why she freed you."

The amber ceiling light flashed and the siren sounded to indicate they were about to take off. Jake climbed into his bunk and strapped himself in, ready for departure. He would be glad to get away from those old-fashioned two-way radios. It had made him feel vulnerable having his eye implants messed up so easily. He had taken his vision for granted while he lived with the cyber-monks over the last eleven years.

Nichelle eased the *Dark Horse* out of the docking bay and away from Papa Don's spaceport. Jake was the first to release his straps. He wanted to see the illegal spaceport one more time before it disappeared from view. In the back of his mind, he kept thinking about the girl, Kella. Why was it so hard, talking to girls? If only he had been able to apologize to her. It wasn't like she needed any more reasons to be miserable, locked up in that cell.

Jake strapped on his makeshift gravity shoes and walked across the room to the porthole window. He was surprised to see a familiar shape in the distance.

"It's the naval warship," he said. "The one from Remota."

"What?" Callidus drifted over from his bunk. "What is that doing here?"

"Do you think it's following us?" asked Capio.

Granny Leatherhead appeared in the door with Farid.

"Have you seen the super-destroyer?" she croaked. "That's the ISS *Colossus*, the most powerful Interstellar Spaceship in the fleet, under the direct command of Admiral Algor Nex."

"How come I've never heard of it?" asked Jake.

"It's new," she said. "It was only launched a few weeks ago."

"Admiral Nex, eh?" Callidus stroked his stubble. "I haven't heard that name for a while."

"Who is he?" asked Jake.

"A very powerful man who controls a whole fleet of naval warships," said Callidus. "But everyone knows he takes his orders from the Galactic Trade Corporation."

"He's a despicable space devil who's responsible for the deaths of many good pirates," Granny Leatherhead said, and spat. "I've never come across a more vile or vicious villain in the seven solar systems. They say that his eyes are as black as his soul. I'm sure he would love to take down the infamous Space Dogs."

"Do you think he's following us?" asked Jake. "He must be pretty desperate if he's prepared to get close to that nebula cloud."

"I doubt he's looking for me and my crew," said Granny Leatherhead. "Why now, when we've evaded capture for so long? No, he must be searching for something else, or someone else."

They all turned to Jake.

"Me? Why does everyone want me?"

"Word must be getting around," said Callidus, "that you're the boy from Altus."

"What are we going to do?" asked Jake.

"We're going to get our rusty old butt out of here, that's what," said Granny Leatherhead. "I hope the systems on ISS *Colossus* have been scrambled by the Tego Nebula and they won't notice us leaving."

"Where are we heading?" asked Capio.

Granny Leatherhead looked expectantly at Callidus.

"I was hoping Jake's pendant would show us the way to Altus," he said. "If only we knew where to find the Altian shipwreck. At least that might contain some more clues, but I've been looking for it for years and so far I've drawn a blank."

"A shipwreck, eh?" Granny Leatherhead raised an eyebrow. "I know a service port where the salvage crews hang out. It's a filthy little joint a few days away, but if anyone has heard about an old wreck, it will be those scurvy-skinned scroungers."

"It's worth a try," said Callidus, watching the naval warship through the porthole window. "But the quicker we get there, the better."

Chapter 10

Special Cargo

Jake returned to the engine room the next morning. He was still thinking about the naval warship. Was the ISS *Colossus* following them? He found it hard to concentrate on his chores, which included feeding Squawk, cleaning tools, greasing the pistons, and making pots of tea.

In the afternoon, Scargus gave him a lesson with the cutlass, showing him how to defend himself and make the most of zero gravity. Jake was getting used to the weapon and had already mastered several basic moves.

"You're a natural, lad," said Scargus, as Jake disarmed him for the third time. "Was your father a swordsman?"

"No idea." Jake rested the cutlass.

"You're doing really well," said Manik, watching from the sofa. "I've never seen such fast reactions."

"It's not all about speed." Scargus checked the

clock on the wall. "You'd better be off, Jake. It's almost time for dinner."

"You call that mushy stuff dinner? I don't know how you can eat it for weeks on end."

Scargus laughed. "It used to be a lot worse when I was a lad."

Jake stroked Squawk and opened the hatch door. "Thanks for the lesson. I'll see you both tomorrow."

"Bye, Jake," said Manik.

"Keep practicing your footwork," urged Scargus.

Jake left the engine room and walked back to the guest quarters. For the first time since the attack on the monastery, he realized he was in a good mood. He started to sing a space shanty that Manik had taught him:

> *Take me to the launchpad, boy,*
> *Load me up and strap me in,*
> *Life among the stars, ahoy,*
> *Proud to be space pirate kin.*
> *Free to roam, away we cast,*
> *Dogs of space will always win,*
> *Never forget times gone past,*
> *Proud to be space pirate kin.*

*

Jake arrived at his door and stopped. What was that noise? Was someone else singing? He went to the opposite hatch and listened. There was no doubt about it. Somebody was singing on the other side and it didn't sound like the crew.

"Hello?" Jake pressed release and the hatch opened.

A song more elegant than any space shanty enchanted his ears. He entered the room, his curiosity burning.

"Hello?" he repeated.

A young girl floated near the ceiling with her eyes closed. Her long black hair gently swirled round her face like a funeral veil. It was the girl from Papa Don's prison block. What was she doing aboard the *Dark Horse*? "Kella?"

The girl jumped. Her face sank when she saw Jake standing by the door.

"Oh, it's you. What are you doing here?"

"I was going to ask you the same question."

"Isn't it obvious?" she said haughtily. "I've been kidnapped."

"Kidnapped?"

"By the space mafia. But now it looks as though I've been sold to common pirates." Kella frowned at Jake. "Are you one of them?"

"No, I'm just a passenger."

"I suppose you don't look much like a space-jacker."

"What do you mean by that?" asked Jake. "I could be a pirate if I wanted."

Kella rolled her eyes. "Whatever you say, tough guy."

Jake was determined not to get drawn into another argument. "I can't believe you've been kidnapped. That's awful."

"What do you care?"

"Look, I'm sorry, okay," he apologized. "I didn't mean to upset you back in the prison block."

"It's all right for you," said Kella. "At least you're allowed out of your room."

"Is there something I can do to help?"

"Do you have any money?"

Jake looked blankly at her.

"I'm being held for ransom," she explained. "My family owns a crystal mine in the sixth solar system. It's run by my older sister, Jeyne."

"So why doesn't she pay for your release? I thought the Galactic Trade Corporation had loads of money."

"Jeyne doesn't work for those wretches," said Kella irritably. "Her mine is far more ethical than those corporate death pits. I don't know why she hasn't paid the ransom yet. It's been weeks."

"I'm sure there's a good reason."

"Oh yeah?" she said. "So why have they moved me onto a pirate ship?"

It suddenly dawned on Jake. "You must be the cargo."

"The what?"

"We stopped at Papa Don's to pick up some special cargo," he explained. "I assumed it was illegal weapons or stolen goods, but the crew must have been referring to you."

"Is that all I am to these people? Cargo? Just an item to be delivered?"

It wasn't right. Nobody should be treated this way, not even someone as grumpy as Kella. Jake wanted to help, but how? There was no way off the ship and nowhere to hide her.

"Come with me," he said, holding out his hand.

"Where?"

"We're going to see the captain."

Jake grabbed Kella's wrist and pulled her through the air like a human balloon. Ignoring her objections, he towed her out of the room, along the corridor, and up the metal staircase.

"I don't like this," she said, when they reached the top deck. "We're going to get into trouble."

"It's okay," he assured her. "I'm always in trouble."

Without hesitation, Jake stormed onto the bridge and straight into the back of Kodan, bouncing off the huge man and almost letting go of Kella. Kodan spun around and glared at the pair of them. Granny Leatherhead, Farid, and Nichelle also turned to see what was happening.

"Hey," said Farid. "What are you two doing up here?"

Jake marched into the center of the room.

"How can you abduct this girl?" he asked angrily. "I thought you were pirates, not kidnappers."

"Ah, I see you've met our other passenger," croaked Granny Leatherhead. "Well done, my dim-witted detective, you've managed to stick your nose into our business yet again."

"Kella's not a passenger," said Jake. "I know she's your 'special cargo' and she's being held for ransom."

"Stand down, you pocket-size pest," barked Granny Leatherhead. "How dare you step onto my bridge and make such accusations? We haven't abducted anyone. If you must know, the space mafia took Kella away from her family, but before they could collect the ransom, her sister went and got herself arrested by the Interstellar Navy."

"Jeyne's been arrested?" Kella looked shocked. "But she's not a criminal."

"Maybe she is and maybe she isn't, dear," said Granny Leatherhead. "The truth doesn't matter when you've got something that the Galactic Trade Corporation wants. Those manipulative maggots will do anything to get their hands on crystal mines, including making up evidence and framing people."

"Will I ever see her again?"

"I doubt it," said Granny Leatherhead. "When old Papa Don realized he wasn't going to get his money, he wanted you off his spaceport fast, which is why he's paying us to take you to a distant colony, where you'll be sold as a slave."

Jake was horrified.

"Is this what the infamous Space Dogs have become?" He turned to Farid and Nichelle, who avoided his eyes. "Slave traders?"

Granny Leatherhead stormed over to Jake and pressed her face up to his, choking him with her foul breath.

"You insolent space pup," she growled, her leather eye patch rubbing against his brow. "Nobody makes demands on my bridge, do you hear me? Nobody. Especially not some purple-eyed orphan boy."

Jake held his ground and stared her out. He was half Granny Leatherhead's size and a fraction of her age, but he was determined not to let her bully them.

The standoff showed no sign of ending, when Farid interrupted.

"Captain, you need to see this."

Granny Leatherhead gave a final scowl and pulled away. Jake glanced up at Kella, who smiled at him. For the first time, he noticed how pretty she looked, when she wasn't frowning.

"What is it, Farid?" snapped Granny Leatherhead.

"The scanners have picked up an alloy structure on the surface of a nearby asteroid. It's a shipwreck."

The *Dark Horse* drew closer to the giant asteroid, but keeping enough distance to avoid its gravitational pull. An image of the shipwreck appeared on the computer display. It looked old and derelict, like a metal carcass resting on the rocky surface. The crew were so busy scanning the shipwreck, they forgot about Jake and Kella, who stood silently watching. Jake stared at the damaged hull, wondering if the crew had escaped or if their bodies were still trapped inside.

"We pass wrecks all the time," croaked Granny Leatherhead. "What's so special about this one?"

"I don't recognize the design," said Farid, squinting at the display screen. "It could be the Altian shipwreck."

Jake's heart leaped. Was it possible that this wreck had come from his home planet? Had they stumbled across his father's ship?

"Woorak, fetch me Callidus. I want him on the bridge now," ordered Granny Leatherhead over the intercom.

A few minutes later Woorak appeared in the doorway with Callidus, who was now wearing gravity boots. The fortune seeker seemed pleased to be out of his room, but also curious as to why he had been summoned. He observed the shipwreck with interest.

"Is it Altian?" asked Granny Leatherhead, getting straight to the point.

"I don't think so," said Callidus. "None of its markings look like the design on Jake's pendant."

"Where could it be from then?" asked Jake, his hopes fading fast.

"I don't know. It could be alien."

"Alien?" scoffed Nichelle. "It's been decades since anyone came into contact with a new species, let alone one capable of space flight."

"In that case, we're due for another encounter," said Callidus. "If it's not a known alien ship, then it could be a species we haven't met yet. Not that we'll find any survivors on this wreck."

"Don't be so sure, clever clogs." Granny Leatherhead pointed to a small flashing light on one of the displays. "We're detecting a faint energy reading and I want to find out what's causing it."

"The sensors have picked up a mild heat signature inside the wreck," Farid said, elaborating. "It must be something that doesn't require oxygen, like a computer or a mechanical device."

Jake found it incredible that anything could be working on such a lifeless ruin.

"The hull appears intact with no sign of tampering," continued the first mate, "which means there could still be treasure on board, or worst case, spare parts to salvage."

"It's rare to find an unclaimed wreck," said Granny Leatherhead. "I want to make the most of this opportunity, but it'll be tricky gaining access and removing the goods from this distance."

"It would be a dangerous mission even for a trained salvage team," agreed Callidus. "Who are you sending over there?"

"You," she cackled. "You and your cowardly companion, Capio. I want you to check it out for us."

"Wait a minute. That's not part of our deal," said Callidus.

"Tough luck, buddy," she croaked, drawing her laser pistol. "I make the rules around here and I say you're going. You can take Jake with you as well. A stroll in space should cool his heels."

"But we don't have time for this," protested Jake. "What about Altus? What about the ISS *Colossus*?"

"We'll make time," said Granny Leatherhead. "Your planet will have to wait."

Jake didn't like the idea of entering a sealed space tomb. Kella tightened her grip around his hand. He looked into her emerald-green eyes and found them full of concern.

"It's okay," he lied. "I'll be back before you know it."

Chapter 11

Ghost Ship

Callidus and Jake were escorted to the air lock on the side of the ship, where Capio was waiting. Maaka Metal Head showed them how their space suits operated and gave them useful tips for surviving in space, such as how to breathe properly and monitor their heart rates.

Jake was too short even for the smallest space suit, so Maaka customized one using plastic clips and sticky tape. It looked ridiculous, but at least it would keep him alive outside. Maaka secured the space helmet and gave Jake a thumbs-up through the visor. Jake found it strange breathing in the cold compressed air, though it tasted fresher than the stale stuff they pumped around the ship.

"Have you ever done this before, Cal?" he asked Callidus, surprised to hear his own voice echoing inside the helmet.

"Yes, I've done a few space walks in my time," said the fortune seeker, securing his space helmet and adjusting the built-in communicator. "Don't worry. Stick with me and you'll be okay."

"That's if we don't get eaten by space monsters," grumbled Capio, stuffing himself into his space suit.

"It'll be fine," insisted Callidus. "Think of it as an adventure. Who knows what we might find."

Jake was trying his best not to imagine what could be waiting for them aboard the wreck. He liked the idea of discovering treasure, but his mind kept producing images of dead crewmen and alien monsters.

"What does space smell like?" he asked.

"No one knows for sure," said Callidus. "A few people claim it has a salty odor similar to ocean water, while others reckon it's more sulfurous like gunpowder. But if anyone tried exposing their nose to space, they would freeze to death before they smelled anything."

"Right, it's time," interrupted Maaka, stepping outside the air lock. "Keep an eye out for each other and don't let go of the tow cable."

He closed the inner door and winked at them through a small window. The tow cable had been fired from the *Dark Horse* to connect the ship to the giant asteroid. Callidus, Capio, and Jake would use the thick wire to pull themselves across to the ship-wreck. As a safety precaution, they had to clip themselves to the tow cable using thinner wires, known as lifelines, which were attached to their space suits.

Jake turned to face the outer air lock door, his heart thumping in nervous anticipation. The space boots were too large for his feet, but they were far more effective at keeping him grounded than the homemade gravity shoes. He started to wonder if Granny Leatherhead was playing a joke on them, when two amber lights flashed on the ceiling.

"Warning, air lock door opening," announced a speaker on the wall.

Jake's pulse doubled and his eyes wedged open. All he could think about was the lack of air outside the ship. There was nothing except ice-cold empty space.

The huge outer door cracked open, allowing all the oxygen in the air lock to escape, along with a layer of dust and some bits of rubbish. Jake's body was pulled forward by an invisible force, but his boots kept him firmly anchored. Callidus and Capio used wall straps to steady themselves, while waiting to exit the ship.

The door finished opening and Callidus walked to the edge of the air lock. He located the tow cable and signaled for the others to join him. Jake took a deep breath and stepped forward, wrenching his magnetic soles from the metal floor. In a few paces, he was standing face-to-face with outer space. His purple eyes bathed in the light of a billion stars.

"Magnifty."

The universe was vast and spectacular. It made him feel small and insignificant, like a tadpole about to swim in the ocean. His legs weakened as he thought about leaving the air lock. He knew there was no gravity outside, but he couldn't help feeling as though he might fall. The trick with heights was to avoid looking down, he told himself—except there was no such thing as up or down in space.

"I'll go first," said Callidus through the helmet communicator. "Jake, you follow next, and Capio, you bring up the rear."

"Do we have to do this?" Capio whined.

"Yes," said Callidus, clipping his lifeline to the tow cable and stepping out of the air lock. "Unless you want to try it without a space suit?"

Jake waited until Callidus was clear before reaching up and attaching his own lifeline to the tow cable. His hands were only just able to grip the thick wire through his bulky gloves, but he was determined to prove himself. Ignoring the sick feeling in his stomach, he leaned forward and stepped out of the airlock, his heart now beating like a machine gun as he drifted into space.

"Keep hold of that tow cable," instructed Callidus, checking behind him. "That's good, Jake, very good. Just watch out for stray asteroids."

Jake moved along the wire one hand at a time. He wasn't as fast as Callidus, but he did his best to keep up, while Capio followed behind, still complaining.

"It's not ethical to do favors for space pirates," muttered Capio. "My mother would be so ashamed."

It was surprisingly hard work and Jake's arms soon grew tired. He was also feeling space sick, but resisted the urge to throw up inside his helmet. This was a common reaction to floating in space, brought on by the strange sensation of having nothing beneath your feet and still not falling. Jake tried to focus on the crumpled shipwreck ahead.

"Watch out," shouted Callidus.

Jake looked up and saw a small rock hurtling toward him. He dived out of the way and lost his grip on the tow cable, tumbling backward into space. The rock shot over his head, missing him by inches as he turned a full somersault. Jake reached back for the cable, swiping at it with both hands, but it had already slipped beyond his grasp.

"Help!" he cried, powerless to stop himself drifting away.

"Keep calm," said Callidus, his voice clear inside Jake's helmet.

Keep calm? How was he supposed to keep calm when he was spiraling out of control? Was this how his father had felt all those years ago, when he'd been lost in the asteroid field?

"Cal—" he began, but then something tugged at his side.

Jake looked down to find a thin wire attached to his space suit. His lifeline, he was saved!

Feeling foolish, he used it to guide him back to the tow cable, which he hugged like an old friend.

The rest of the journey seemed to take forever. When they finally made contact with the shipwreck, Jake was ready to collapse.

"How are your arms?" asked Callidus, clearing a patch of space barnacles with his boots.

"Twice as long as when we started, but I'll be okay."

Callidus disconnected himself from the tow cable and explored the damaged outer surface, searching the scarred metal for a way inside. It didn't take him long to locate the doors and open them with laser cutters. The three of them entered the ship and activated their helmet lamps.

"What peculiar writing." Capio shone his light at a sign on the wall.

"I don't recognize it at all," said Callidus, wiping a layer of condensation off the sign with his glove.

There was something eerie about entering the shipwreck. It was like disturbing a grave or raiding a tomb.

"That's strange," said Callidus, as they ventured deeper inside the wreckage. "The internal doors have all been manually opened, but there were no signs of forced entry outside."

They entered a wide corridor, which contained more writing, this time etched on to the wall. Jake was relieved that there weren't any monsters waiting for them. He wasn't the only one feeling spooked.

"Do you believe in ghosts?" asked Capio. "You know, shipmates who die in space and endlessly roam the cosmos in search of a decent burial."

"Be quiet," snapped Callidus. "There are no such things as ghost ships."

"I'm sorry, Cal, but I can't help it. This wreck is giving me the creeps."

"Capio—" Callidus stopped and listened. "What was that noise?"

No one moved.

"I didn't hear anything," whispered Capio. "Are you trying to scare me?"

"No, I definitely heard something moving," said Callidus.

"The energy reading?" guessed Jake.

"It's probably something mobile, like a guard robot or maintenance android." Callidus shone his light up the corridor. "I just hope it's friendly."

The three of them listened for further clues, but there was nothing except silence. Jake longed to be back aboard the *Dark Horse*.

"Ahoy there," echoed Farid's voice inside their helmets. "How's it going?"

"Fine, thanks," said Callidus softly, turning down his helmet communicator. "But this isn't a good time."

"What's going on?" asked the first mate. "Why are you whispering?"

"We heard something moving," said Callidus. "We're going to investigate."

"We are?" choked Capio.

A loud crash up the corridor made them all jump.

"What was that?" asked Farid.

"Ghosts," whimpered Capio. "I knew this wreck was haunted. Let's get out of here."

"Over there," said Callidus, catching something green moving with his light.

"What is it?" asked Jake, unable to make out the shape before it disappeared through a doorway.

"I don't know," said Callidus, storming up the corridor. "But we're going to find out."

"Are you crazy?" hissed Capio. "I'm not going after that thing."

"Fine, stay there."

Jake shared Capio's reluctance, but decided that it would be safer with the fortune seeker. He clomped up the corridor after him, struggling to keep up in his oversized suit. It wasn't long before he lost sight of Callidus. Jake stopped in a circular room containing three doors.

"Cal?" he called out in the darkness. "Are you there?"

Nobody answered.

"Capio?"

Nobody answered.

"Farid?" He fiddled with his helmet communicator, hoping to hear a familiar voice.

Nobody answered.

Jake was lost again, only this time in a shipwreck on an asteroid. He stood in the center of the room, staring at the three doors, when something moved behind him. Jake turned and came face-to-face with the green shape.

Capio was right. They had boarded a ghost ship.

Chapter 12

Alien Encounter

Jake stared at the tattered green space suit hovering in the shadows, transfixed with fear. He half expected to see a skull or two glowing eyes glaring at him from behind the dusty visor. To his horror, the figure drew nearer, arms outstretched and feet suspended above the ground, casting a terrifying shadow against the curved wall.

A shadow? Since when did ghosts have shadows?

"Hey, you're no space ghoul," shouted Jake. "I'm warning you, don't come any closer."

The space suit stopped moving and lingered in the air. Its arms lowered and its head tilted curiously to the side. Jake noticed the unusual suit design. Apart from the lime-green color, it was made out of a skin-like material, which looked tighter and more flexible than their space suits.

"Who you?" asked the figure in a muffled voice. "Why you on my ship?"

"Your ship?" said Jake. "I thought this was an abandoned wreck."

The figure went to speak again but was interrupted when Callidus burst into the room, wielding a metal bar.

"There you are," he said. "I've got you now."

"Wait," cried Jake, stepping in front of the tattered space suit.

"Get out of the way," warned Callidus.

"No, listen to me," said Jake, not moving. "This isn't a ghost, or a monster, or a robot. It's the owner of the spaceship."

"The owner?" Callidus lowered the metal bar.

Jake turned back to the floating figure. "I'm sorry, we didn't mean to scare you. My name's Jake Cutler and this is Callidus Stone. Who are you?"

The figure reached up and wiped the dust off its visor, revealing the face of a young alien boy. His pale lilac skin had not been washed for some time, and his wide turquoise eyes blinked nervously.

"My name Nanoo," he said. "I not mean to run away. It long time since anyone here. I thinking you might hurt me."

"Where are you from?" asked Callidus, releasing the metal bar. "I've never seen a vessel like this before."

"I from planet Taan-Centaur, many galaxies away. This was exploration ship. My parents seek new worlds. We on scientific mission when we lose control and crash. My parents and crew die, but I living here since accident, almost one year."

"You've been living in this wreck for a year!" exclaimed Callidus. "How is that possible?"

"Life support still work after crash, but it broken two weeks ago and air run out. I wear space suit to breathe now, but oxygen tanks almost gone, so I nearly a ghost."

Callidus remained suspicious. "If you're an alien from another galaxy, how can you speak our language?"

"My people called Novu. I learn your language from listening to data files. My parents collect samples of your speaking from far away. Novu talk is different."

Nanoo spoke to them in his native language, using a mixture of clicks and whistles. It sounded like a tap-dancing tea kettle to Jake.

"I'm sorry about the crash," said Jake. "It must have been awful living here on your own. I'm glad we found you before it was too late."

Nanoo's eyes grew wider. "You help me?"

"Now hold on a minute," said Callidus, holding

up his hands. "No offense, Nanoo, but we can't just take anyone with us."

"Why not?" asked Jake. "We can't leave him here to die."

"I'm sorry, but for all we know, he could be dangerous," said Callidus. "After all, we only have his word for what happened."

"Dangerous?" Jake couldn't believe his ears. "He's just a boy, like me, a shipwrecked boy who's lost his parents."

Nanoo looked worried. "Please take me. I not want to be by self."

Callidus studied the young Novu carefully. "Where are the remains of your parents and the crew?"

"I unable to keep them on ship and no way to burn them, so I place bodies inside specimen crates and send into space. I now child without parents."

"The word you're looking for is *orphan*," said Jake, having worn that label himself for eleven years.

"What about the rest of your people?" asked Callidus. "Will others come looking for you?"

"No likely," said Nanoo. "We not due home for one more year. No one know we crash. Distress beacon damage on impact. Most equipment damage. No engine, no communicator, no escape pod. It all broken."

Footsteps approached the door.

"Hello?" called out Capio nervously. "Is anyone there?"

Nanoo retreated behind Jake.

"Don't be afraid," said Callidus. "That's Capio and he's not even slightly dangerous."

"Cal, is that you?" Capio shone his light through the doorway.

"Yes, we're in here," said the fortune seeker. "I wondered when you would show up."

Capio entered the room and jumped.

"Look out behind you, Jake!" he shrieked. "It's the ghost, run for your life!"

"It's okay," said Jake. "This is Nanoo and he's not dead."

"What did you say?" Capio was already halfway out of the door. "Not dead? So how come he's floating there with lilac skin?"

Nanoo slid out from behind Jake. "I always this color. I alien. I remove magnets from boots when gravity drive damage, because being weightless save energy."

He lifted up his feet to show where the magnets had been, while Callidus reported back to the *Dark Horse*.

"Ahoy, Farid, are you there?"

"Ahoy, shipwreckers," said the first mate. "Have you found anything yet?"

"Yes, we've got a surprise for Granny Leatherhead." Callidus smiled. "We'll finish up and head back over."

"Okay, but don't be long; the captain is getting impatient."

Nanoo gave Jake, Callidus, and Capio a quick tour of his vessel. Its sleek design and innovative engineering made the *Dark Horse* seem like a clumsy clockwork relic. There was no obvious treasure on board, only scientific notes and samples stored on data files. Nanoo placed these into a bag, along with his clothes and several gadgets that looked like they belonged to a dentist.

"Right, time to go," said Callidus, checking his wrist computer.

Nanoo stiffened in the air.

"Are you okay?" asked Jake.

"I not sure," said Nanoo. "It long time since I go outside."

Jake tried to imagine what it must be like for Nanoo. How would any of them feel?

"It'll be okay," he said. "I'll look out for you."

Nanoo drifted to the nearest wall and touched it with his hand. "Good-bye, friend. Rest well."

The four of them headed to the air lock. There were no spare lifelines, so Jake tied himself to Nanoo using his space suit belt. It wasn't ideal, but it would stop the Novu boy from floating away.

If Jake thought the outbound journey was tough, having someone strapped to him made the return trip even harder. By the time they reached the *Dark Horse*, he felt as though his arms would fall off. With a final burst of energy, Jake reached out and grasped the edge of the air lock, but he was too weak to pull himself aboard. He hung there for a moment, shattered, unable to move, Nanoo still floating beside him. Callidus reached down and dragged them both inside, while Capio pushed from behind.

"Well done," said Callidus, tapping on Jake's visor. "You made it."

Jake held up a shaking thumb. "Thanks."

Nanoo's turquoise eyes scanned the inside of the cargo hauler, like a historian examining an ancient artifact. The huge outer door closed and the oxygen levels restored. As they removed their helmets and space suits, the inner door slid open and Granny Leatherhead stomped into the air lock, accompanied by Maaka and Kodan.

"What took you ugly upstarts so long and where's my treasure?" she croaked, before noticing Nanoo. "Who are you?"

Nanoo stood holding his helmet. His long face and bald head made him look like a jelly bean. "My name Nanoo. Thank you for save me."

"He's from the shipwreck," said Jake. "He's been living there for almost a year, but his oxygen was about to run out."

"Not another stray," she groaned. "How many more people can we squeeze onto this ship? Is he sick? He looks a little off color."

"He's from a distant planet called Taan-Centaur," said Callidus. "His people are called the Novu, but I've never come across them."

"He's an alien?" Granny Leatherhead covered her mouth. "How do you know he's not carrying any germs? I want him quarantined for twenty-four hours before we let him anywhere near the guest quarters."

"You mean he can stay?" Jake was half expecting Nanoo to be thrown back into space.

"What? If he must—"

"Thanks, Captain. You won't regret it."

Kodan escorted Nanoo to the medical bay, where he could be observed. There had only been three alien encounters in history and one of them had resulted in a new supervirus, so Granny Leatherhead wasn't taking any chances.

"I hope he wasn't all you brought back with you," she croaked. "What else did you find?"

"Not much," said Callidus, passing his space suit to Maaka. "There was no treasure or useful supplies, only a few data files and some alien gadgets. Everything else was damaged."

"No treasure? No supplies? Curse you good-for-nothing numbskulls, can't you do anything right? I don't know why you bothered coming back."

"We nearly didn't, you old bag," muttered Capio.

"What was that?" she demanded.

"Um, I said, if we didn't, it would have been too bad."

Granny Leatherhead's expression turned so bitter it looked as though she had swallowed a lemon. "I'm warning you, you miserable morons," she said. "We still haven't found any more clues to the location of Altus and I'm running out of patience. If this service port is another dead end, there's going to be trouble."

Granny Leatherhead swept out of the air lock and up the corridor. Jake stood there for a moment, waiting for her footsteps to fade. What did she mean by trouble? What if Altus was just a children's story after all?

At least the captain was letting Nanoo stay on the ship. Jake looked forward to the next day, when the Novu boy would be let out of quarantine. With aching muscles, he followed Callidus and Capio back to their quarters to rest. Jake was exhausted, but he would never forget his first space walk, the shipwreck, and the alien boy.

Chapter 13

The Service Port

The *Dark Horse* traveled for two more days to the service port where the salvage crews hung out. During that time Nanoo was given the all-clear and released from quarantine. Jake waited for him in the corridor.

"I not like being alone in there," said Nanoo, "but at least I remove space suit."

Jake noticed Nanoo was wearing fresh clothes made of a similar skin-like material. He showed Nanoo back to the guest quarters and introduced him to Kella, who was intrigued to meet her first Novu. Nanoo was equally curious about his rescuers and asked lots of questions. Jake did his best to provide a history of their galaxy, explaining how there were seven solar systems containing populated planets, most of which were united by a corrupt Interstellar Government and protected by a powerful Interstellar Navy.

"I suppose Altus is an independent colony, like the planet I grew up on, Remota."

"We Novu live only on Taan-Centaur," said Nanoo. "But I wanting to visit other worlds. Altus sound amazing."

"Well, let's hope the salvage crews can point us in the right direction." Kella looked at Jake. "We'd all like to see Altus and its crystal moons."

The three of them talked for hours about random subjects, covering everything from their hobbies to their favorite food. Jake was enjoying hanging out with people his own age for the first time in his life. He was beginning to realize what he'd been missing.

"You sleeping every night?" said Nanoo. "That strange."

"Why, how often do you sleep?" asked Kella.

"Novu sleeping one every three days. We work, not rest."

"Hey, what are those cuts on your neck?" asked Jake. "Are they gills to help you breathe underwater?"

"Not gills." Nanoo peeled open one of the slits. "These for eat and drink. You not have them?"

"No way, that's gross. I can't believe you pour stuff straight into your neck." Jake pulled a face as he imagined how it must feel. "We use our mouths for that."

"Your mouths?" Nanoo made a similar expression. "My mouth is for talk and breathe only."

"What about kissing?" asked Kella.

Nanoo's face turned dark lilac and Jake burst out laughing. It was the first time he'd laughed in weeks and it felt good. Kella joined in, but Nanoo failed to see the funny side.

"I know something that will cheer you up, Nanoo," said Jake, grabbing their wrists.

He towed his new friends along the corridor to the engine room, so he could introduce them to Scargus and Manik.

"We'd better not get caught, Jake," said Kella. "I'm still supposed to be confined to my room."

"Come on, where's your sense of adventure?"

Scargus and Manik seemed pleased to have visitors. Nanoo had his first-ever cup of tea and Kella got to feed Squawk the parrot. Manik found more magnets and transformed their footwear into gravity shoes, as she had done for Jake. In return, Nanoo showed her how to double the engine's efficiency, giving the ship more power while using less fuel.

"Hey, that's really smart," said Manik, holding up his scribbled notes and diagrams.

Nanoo beamed. "Thanks, it just shame I not as good with language as technology. Engines are magnafty."

"I think you mean magnifty," corrected Jake.

"Keep practicing," said Scargus. "I doubt we could speak Novu that well."

"How about you, Kella?" asked Manik. "Do you have any special talents?"

"I'm not great with languages or technology, but I like to sing and I'm pretty good with crystals."

"What, mining them?" asked Jake.

"No, you astronut. I use crystals to heal people. It's a skill my grandmother taught me." Kella shrugged modestly. "I'm not as good as she is, but I can still heal cuts and bruises in hours, instead of days."

"Impressive," said Manik. "I've heard of crystal healers, but you're the first I've met."

"It's not something I normally tell people." Kella frowned. "Most United Worlds think crystal healing is a form of witchcraft. I was bullied at school when the other kids found out about my grandmother. But those people don't like independent colonists or space pirates either."

"Well, I think crystal healing sounds pretty magnifty," said Jake.

"Me too," agreed Manik. "We could use a healer like you. Doctor Yu, the ship's medic, got himself arrested a couple of months ago."

"Sorry, but I can't help you," said Kella with a shrug. "I'm just cargo. I shouldn't even be out of my room."

146

The engine-room door opened and Woorak entered. "We're approaching the service p-p-port. The captain wants you b-b-back in your quarters and strapped in t-t-tight."

"Why?" asked Jake. "Is it going to be a rough landing?"

"No, she just w-w-wants you out of the w-w-way, so you can't get into t-t-trouble."

Jake, Kella, and Nanoo made their way back to the guest quarters. In the corridor, Nanoo admitted feeling overwhelmed to be aboard the *Dark Horse*.

"I not used to busy ship after being by self for so long. At times I feared nobody find me. I not want to be alone again."

"It's okay. We're all afraid of something," said Kella, trying to master her gravity shoes. "I used to play in my family's crystal mine, until I got trapped there overnight. I've been scared of the dark ever since. My sister has always been the brave one, the risk taker, the one who makes our parents proud. I'm pretty sure her only dread is the fear of failing."

"What you think Granny Leatherhead fear?" asked Nanoo.

"Probably her own reflection," said Jake.

When they reached the guest quarters, Nanoo stayed with Kella, so they could keep each other company. Jake returned to his room and climbed into his bunk. He lay there listening to the sound of the cargo hauler docking at the service port. His thoughts drifted back to Altus, the Space Dogs, and the naval warship. He hoped the salvage teams would know where to find his father's shipwreck, otherwise there would be trouble aboard the *Dark Horse*.

Once they had docked, all the crew and passengers gathered in the dining area of the *Dark Horse*, with the exception of Kella. Farid and Kodan volunteered to lead a landing party, keen to prove themselves after the mix-up at Papa Don's.

"Okay," said Granny Leatherhead. "Just make sure you take Callidus, Capio, Jake, and Nanoo with you. I want to rid my ship of guests for a while. It's getting a little crowded."

"What about Kella?" asked Jake.

"The girl stays here," grumped Granny Leatherhead. "Kella's not a guest, she's cargo, and I can't risk her running away."

"I'm sure she'll behave herself," said Jake. "Besides, when we find Altus, you'll be so rich that you won't need to sell her."

"Is that so?" croaked Granny Leatherhead. "And what about Papa Don? I promised him that I would make the girl disappear and he's not the type to forgive easily."

"Since when do pirates keep their promises?" muttered Capio.

"Yeah, I thought you were the infamous Space Dogs and you put the *fear* into *stratosphere*," said Jake, angry at the way Kella was being treated. "It sounds to me like you're the ones who are afraid."

Granny Leatherhead reached for her laser pistol. "Nobody insults a space pirate on their own ship."

Callidus quickly stepped forward to intervene before the captain could shoot Jake.

"Think about it," he said. "Papa Don is probably busy with the Interstellar Navy. If we're lucky, they will have closed down his spaceport by now. I'm sure Kella is the last thing on his mind. I give you my word that we'll keep an eye on her."

"Fine, whatever, take the blasted girl and get off my ship." Granny Leatherhead waved her hands above her head. "Just go, before I throttle the lot of you."

Farid hurried everyone to the air lock, while Kodan fetched Kella.

"Now, listen up," said the first mate. "I don't want any trouble this time, so don't go looking for it. We're just going to talk with some salvage crews and then come straight back to the ship. Nice and simple, no messing about. Is that clear?"

Everyone nodded, but Jake was starting to realize how few things were "nice and simple" when it came to being a space pirate. Trouble insisted on looking for them, not the other way around.

Farid led the landing party out of the air lock and on to an industrial walkway inside the service port. It was filled with engineers, mechanics, and salvage crews, who meandered around in dirty overalls, carrying bulky tools and munching on greasy snacks. The air was contaminated with the smell of spray paint and solder fumes.

"It's very . . . basic," said Callidus.

Capio had a different word for it. "What a dump."

The service port was a functional place, used for building and repairing spacecraft, as well as selling fuel and supplies. It wasn't as large or impressive as Papa Don's illegal spaceport, but at least there were fewer space pirates. After passing several maintenance bays and supply shops, they located the canteen where the salvage teams hung out while waiting for their next job.

Farid paused by the entrance door. "Now what?"

"We make some inquiries," said Callidus. "But it will be quicker if we split up. I suggest that Jake comes with me, Nanoo goes with Capio, and Kella stays with Farid and Kodan."

Jake followed Callidus into the canteen, where rough-looking crews were crammed around small tables. Most of them were watching intergalactic sports on big screens or staring out of the huge porthole windows. A house robot poured drinks and served food behind a chipped wooden counter.

Callidus approached the first table, but the captain just laughed when he mentioned Altus.

"Altian shipwrecks?" snorted the bearded man, flicking a roasted nut into his mouth. "Why don't you ask the space goblins?"

Callidus moved to the next crew, who also mocked him. Jake could tell from the expressions on their faces that Capio and the others weren't having much luck either. He was starting to wonder if anyone would take them seriously, when Callidus spoke to an old pilot at the counter.

"You should ask Baden," said the pilot, thumbing in the direction of a table near the window. "He's the scruffy one in orange. Baden reckons Altus exists, but then again, he spends so much time in deep space, he probably believes in the moon fairy as well."

Callidus and Jake strolled over to the table, where four people were playing cards. Baden wore a dirty orange exploration suit and his mouth was stuffed with chewing gum. His three shipmates were dressed in T-shirts and loose overalls. They must have been sitting there for some time, judging by the number of cups on the table.

"What can we do for you?" asked Baden, without looking up. "We only work for crystals."

"I'm after information," said Callidus. "It's about a shipwreck."

"What wreck?" Baden remained engrossed in the game. "We've salvaged loads of wrecks over the years."

"This one is special," insisted Callidus, leaning over the table. "It's a ship from Altus."

This time, nobody laughed.

Chapter 14

The Reunion

Baden eyed Callidus suspiciously. "Did one of the other crews put you up to this?"

"No. They reckon we're crazy for asking about Altus."

Baden put down his cards and swept back his faded brown hair. "Okay, you've got my attention."

Callidus pulled up a seat and signaled for Jake to do the same.

"What's this, a family outing?" asked Baden, then he added, "Hey, nice implants, kiddo."

"My name is Jake."

"Pleased to meet you. I'm Baden Scott, captain of the *Rough Diamond II*, and this is my crew: Gunnar, Reinhart, and our pilot, Kiki."

"What happened to the first *Rough Diamond*?" asked Jake.

"That's a long story." Baden rubbed a scar on his stubbly chin. "It involves the space mafia, a golden sword, and a game of Reus roulette."

"What do you know about an Altian wreck?" pressed Callidus.

"We were paid to do a job eleven years ago," said Baden, lowering his voice. "The Interstellar Navy hired us to dispose of a badly damaged wreck near a planet called Remota. It was an unusual ship, unlike anything we've ever salvaged before."

"Unusual how?"

"The design was old-fashioned," said Baden. "You know, like the spaceships you see displayed in museums, only more modern, if that makes sense. I heard someone say it was from Altus, but I thought they were kidding. It was just another job for us."

"Jake, show him your pendant."

Jake pulled out his gold necklace and Baden's eyes flickered with recognition.

Callidus pointed at the three crystals. "Have you seen this design before?"

"Yeah, reckon I have," said Baden. "It was on that shipwreck. Who are you people?"

"Historians," lied Callidus. "We're researching popular myths and we would like to take a look at the wreck, with your permission of course."

"Popular myths?" Baden sounded skeptical. "I'm sorry, but we were instructed to destroy the wreck.

Not that there was much left, only a burned-out hull shot to pieces by laser cannon."

"Laser cannon?" said Jake. "But the ship was caught in a space storm."

Baden searched for a picture on his wrist computer.

"I've seen hundreds of wrecks over the years, most of which were scuttled by space pirates or the Interstellar Navy," he said, holding up an old image of a shipwreck. "I know the difference between asteroid damage and laser cannon fire."

Jake stared at the spacecraft in the photo, its blackened hull blending into the background. It was riddled with holes and looked more like space scrap than a ship. He could just make out the three circles of the Altian symbol carved into the dark metal. It was odd to think that he might have once been aboard that vessel.

"Maybe it got shot up after it crashed," said Callidus. "Someone might have used it for target practice."

"What's wrong with you? Are you blind? That ship was hit by laser cannon, not asteroids," insisted Baden. "I'd stake my reputation on it."

"Why would the Interstellar Navy want to get rid of the remains?" asked Jake.

"No idea." Baden turned off his wrist computer and picked up his cards. "We were paid in unmarked gemstones and told not to ask questions. If that ship was from Altus, they didn't want anyone to find out."

"Could there be more than one Altian wreck?" wondered Callidus.

"How should I know?" Baden almost choked on his gum. "Look, I've told you everything I know. Now if you don't mind, I would like to get back to the game."

Jake was suddenly aware that other people were taking an interest in their conversation. Callidus thanked Baden for his time and stood up to leave, when Capio and Nanoo appeared at the table.

"I heard what salvage man say," said Nanoo excitedly. "I must speak with him."

"What is it now?" Baden caught sight of the lilac-skinned boy. "Hey, are you okay?"

"Yes, I fine," said Nanoo. "You help us, so we help you. I know where you find shipwreck. We not go back, so take what you want. It Novu craft from Taan-Centaur."

Nanoo shared the coordinates of his parents' exploration ship with Baden, who seemed pleased to get an unexpected lead.

"Listen, one piece of advice," said the salvage captain. "Don't let the Interstellar Navy find out you're looking for Altus. It could be the last thing you do."

Callidus, Capio, Jake, and Nanoo joined the others outside the canteen.

"Another dead end?" asked Farid.

"Not this time," said Callidus. "At least we know there was a wreck now."

Jake glanced up the walkway and noticed two people watching them from a distance, but before he could say anything they slipped from view. He had only glimpsed them for a second, but he could have sworn it was Kain and Jala, the crystal hunters from Papa Don's illegal spaceport. What were they doing there?

"Cal, did you see—"

"By the moons of Altus!" barked a gruff voice behind them, making Jake jump. "Is that you, Cutler?"

Jake spun around to see who had spoken. In the corridor stood a disheveled man in a shabby linen coat. His face was hidden beneath long unkempt hair and a scruffy beard. He limped toward them, his arms open wide. Jake stepped cautiously behind Callidus, not wishing to be embraced by a crazed space vagabond.

"I thought I would never see you again," said the

man, his fingers twitching and his nails stained from years of neglect.

"How do you know my name?"

"Jake Cutler? Has it really been eleven years? You look just like your father," said the man. "Are those eye implants?"

Farid placed a hand on his laser pistol and the man stopped.

"Who are you?" asked Callidus. "What do you want?"

The stranger seemed taken aback. His head flicked between Jake and Callidus. "Don't you recognize me?"

"No, sorry," said Jake.

"Is there nothing familiar about this old face?"

"Apparently not," said Callidus impatiently. "I'll ask you one more time, who are you?"

"Amicus," said the man, rubbing his eyes with his knuckles. "Amicus Kent. I'm sorry . . . It's been such a long time and I get so confused . . . But you are Jake Cutler, aren't you? I've been searching for you since I heard about the monastery attack. You caused quite a scene in the canteen back there, asking all those questions."

Amicus brushed the hair from his face, revealing tired eyes and a weathered complexion.

Jake gasped. "You have three scars on your forehead."

"Yes, what of it? Your friend has lilac skin, but do you hear me going on about it?"

"No, you don't understand." Jake's mouth struggled to catch up with his brain. "Father Pius told me the man who dumped me at the monastery eleven years ago had three cuts on his forehead."

"Dumped?" said Amicus. "You weren't dumped. I left you with the cyber-monks for your own good."

The last person Jake had expected to meet in the service port was the stranger from his past, someone who had become almost as mythical as Altus itself. His mind flooded with questions. How should he feel about the man who had saved his life and then abandoned him?

"Why did you leave me?" he asked.

"It would have been too dangerous to take you with me," said Amicus. "You were safer on Remota."

"Yeah? Tell that to the space pirates who attacked the monastery." Jake shook with emotion. "You should have taken me back to Altus, where I belong."

"I'm sorry, but you can never go back."

Farid had heard enough. "I suggest we continue this conversation somewhere more discreet. You never know who might be listening out here."

Wary of Amicus, Jake kept his distance as they returned to the canteen. Kella located a corner table where none of the salvage crews could hear them talk, while Farid ordered drinks, including something apple-flavored for Jake. Amicus slurped his black coffee, as though it was a precious nectar.

"I think you'd better start at the beginning," said Callidus.

The man nodded. "It feels so strange, talking about it like this . . . I knew Jake's parents, Andras and Zara Cutler. Andras is . . . or rather, *was* the ruler of Altus and a great leader. I was his top general and closest friend, but that was eleven years ago."

Jake almost choked on his apple drink. "My dad was the ruler of Altus?"

"One of the greatest, until he was betrayed," said Amicus bitterly. "Now Altus is controlled by a traitor."

"So it's true," whooped Capio. "Altus does exist."

"Oh yes, it exists," said Amicus. "But no outsider must ever discover its location. Andras risked everything to protect its secret and I will do the same if necessary. I've not been homeless all these years for the fun of it."

"What happened on the night of the space storm?" asked Callidus.

"Storm?" said Amicus. "There was no storm. We were attacked. Andras discovered that the Galactic Trade Corporation was searching for our planet. He contacted the Interstellar Navy and offered them ten crates of crystals in return for their protection. Admiral Nex agreed to meet us near Remota, but when we arrived, he demanded that we tell him the location of Altus."

"Andras refused?"

"Yes, of course he did. That's when the Interstellar Navy opened fire, hoping to take us prisoner. We tried to defend ourselves, but our weapons had been sabotaged. As the shields crumbled, Andras ordered me to get Jake to safety. He slipped the gold pendant around his son's neck and went to help the others. I took Jake to an escape pod and abandoned ship. It must have been too late to save the rest of the crew, because I saw Andras leap from the air lock in a space suit, only to drift into an asteroid field."

"I don't understand," said Jake. "Why did you tell Father Pius there was a space storm?"

"I had to lie to protect you. If I had told the truth that night, it would have put you and the cyber-monks in danger. I knew people would come looking for you, Jake, which is why I left you in the monastery. There was less chance of them finding you without me hanging around."

"Why would Andras take his son on such a perilous mission?" wondered Capio.

"He thought it would be safe, a simple exchange with no complications," said Amicus. "Andras kept Jake close to him at all times, because he suspected someone wanted to hurt them. He feared it would be more dangerous to leave Jake behind on Altus."

"Do you know who betrayed you?" asked Farid.

"Jake's uncle, Kear Cutler." Amicus spat out the name, as though it were poison. "He was jealous of Andras and resented his power. Kear must have guessed that the Interstellar Navy would never make a deal with an independent colony. He sabotaged our ship, so he could seize Altus for himself."

"That's terrible," said Kella.

"Why don't you return to Altus?" asked Capio. "If nothing else, you could expose the truth about Kear and see that justice is done."

"Justice?" A dark shadow spread across the Altian's face. "I don't want justice, I want revenge. Kear has committed a crime that can never be forgiven. I'd like nothing better than to make him pay for what he has done, but I have no proof. He would have me arrested the moment I set foot on the planet, and then he might suspect that others have survived. The only reason Jake is still alive today is because Kear thinks we're both dead. Don't you see? I cannot return to Altus without putting Jake in danger."

"Why Kear want to kill Jake?" asked Nanoo.

"Isn't it obvious?" said Amicus. "After Andras, Jake is the rightful ruler of Altus."

Jake's mouth fell open in surprise.

"I figured he was important," said Callidus. "Perhaps the son of a politician, but never the number-one chief Altian."

"Nice one, Jake." Kella sounded impressed. "That's magnifty."

"Hello, majesty." Nanoo grinned and bowed his head.

It was too much. In a single conversation, Jake had discovered that the Interstellar Navy had attacked their ship, his uncle had betrayed his father, and he was the rightful ruler of a world he didn't know.

"I don't want a planet," he said, flustered. "I'm too young to rule anything. I just want my dad back."

"Jake, I know it's hard." Callidus put an arm around his shoulder. "But you must consider the possibility that your father is dead."

Jake shrugged off the arm. "We don't know that."

Amicus exchanged glances with Callidus, before speaking to Jake.

"I've missed your father all of these years," he said earnestly. "I don't know what happened to him that day in the asteroid field, or if my friend will ever return, but whatever the future holds, I know he'll be watching over you."

Jake folded his arms and sank into his seat. He refused to accept that his father was dead, until someone could show him the body.

"At least we still have each other," said Kella.

"Yes, this correct," agreed Nanoo. "It not easy losing parents and living on shipwreck, but now I have friends and hope to see Novu people again."

Jake snorted.

Kella reached out and touched his arm. "Come on, Jake. Every cloud has a silver lining."

"Not *every* cloud," mumbled Amicus.

"What does that mean?" asked Jake, sitting up.

"Nothing, forget it," said the Altian. "Jake, we need to think about where to hide you next."

"But I don't want to hide. I want to find—"

There was a sudden commotion in the canteen and people flocked to the porthole windows.

"What are they looking at?" wondered Callidus.

The fortune seeker stood up and joined the crowd at the nearest porthole, pushing his way to the front. By the time he returned, most of the salvage crews were heading for the entrance.

"It's time to go," said Callidus.

"Why?" asked Capio. "What's going on?"

"It's the ISS *Colossus*."

Chapter 15

Admiral Nex

"What is the Interstellar Navy doing here?" asked Amicus as they hurried from the canteen. "I thought they had their own service ports."

"It's your old friend, Admiral Nex," said Callidus. "We think he's following us."

"That space scum?" Amicus drew a laser pistol from inside his linen coat and tossed a second gun to Callidus. "We should stand and fight. I have a score to settle with the Interstellar Navy."

"A couple of pistols against a warship?" scoffed Capio. "Are you mad?"

Farid stopped by a walkway window and swore out loud.

"The captain must have seen them coming," he said. "The *Dark Horse* has gone."

"She's abandoned us?" exclaimed Jake.

"Never trust a space pirate," said Capio.

The lights in the passageway flashed red and a Klaxon wailed. Plasma rifles and palm grenades rocked the service port, reminding Jake of the night the monastery was attacked, except there would be no secret escape tunnels this time.

"Hey, look over there." Kella pointed down the walkway to a group of mechanics who were being pursued by naval troops in midnight-blue uniforms.

Jake watched in horror as the troops opened fire, cutting the unarmed workers down in a hail of plasma bolts.

"Take cover!" shouted Callidus, pulling Amicus behind a small motorized truck.

Jake crouched next to a barrel, hoping it wasn't full of anything flammable, while Kella pulled Nanoo into a shallow doorway. Capio hid behind a narrow pillar, leaving only Farid and Kodan exposed. The two space pirates drew their weapons and fired at the naval troops, but they were heavily outnumbered.

"No," cried Jake, as Kodan took a hit to his shoulder, followed by another to his leg.

The huge man stumbled backward, blood gushing from his wounds, but still shooting. Next to him, Farid yelled out when a plasma bolt creased the side of his head.

"Stop it," screamed Kella, as more shots ricocheted off the doorway.

"I'll teach them to attack children," growled Amicus, breaking cover.

"No, wait," said Callidus, holding him back. "Get everyone inside the canteen. I'll draw their fire."

The fortune seeker ran across the walkway, shooting his pistol. At the same time, Amicus rolled the motorized truck in front of the canteen entrance, using it as a shield while he led the others to safety. Once they were inside the canteen, Farid and Kodan dropped their weapons and slumped to the floor, their clothes drenched in blood.

The canteen was now empty, except for the house robot clearing glasses. Amicus grabbed one of the largest tables and threw it on to its side, before piling on smaller tables and chairs. It was a crude barricade that wouldn't stop a sneeze in Jake's opinion, let alone plasma rifles and palm grenades.

"This is our first line of defense," said Amicus with a crazed glint in his eye. "We'll hold them here as long as we can, before falling back to the serving counter."

"Is there no other way out?" asked Jake.

"Perhaps, but where would you go? The Interstellar Navy has control of the entire service port. There's nowhere better to stand our ground."

"I thought I said no trouble this time," groaned Farid.

"Jake, lend me your pendant." Kella held out her hand. "I can use the crystals to heal their wounds."

Jake removed his gold pendant and passed it to her. Kella ignored the plasma fire outside and held the object over the two men. Her face was determined and her hand movements were deliberate. Jake had no idea how it was supposed to work, but the bleeding appeared to slow. He had never seen anyone heal with crystals before. In Kella's hands they sparkled brighter than ever.

"Good work, Kella," said Amicus. "But there's not much more we can do here without medical equipment."

The Altian general knelt behind the pile of furniture and took aim at the door. Capio reluctantly joined him, picking up a broken chair leg, while the others crouched low and braced themselves. A few seconds later, Callidus came running into the canteen, his pistol smoking.

"Look out, here they come!" he shouted, throwing himself behind the barricade.

"Just like the old days!" howled Amicus, tasting battle once more.

The squad burst through the door, their plasma rifles blasting. Amicus picked a target and fired, taking out the first trooper with a single shot. Callidus injured another and Capio hurled his chair leg, but it made little difference. The plasma rifles quickly demolished the pile of furniture, showering the floor with debris.

"Fall back to the serving counter," ordered Amicus, as the largest table exploded.

Jake, Kella, Nanoo, and Capio scuttled across the floor, dragging Farid and Kodan behind them. When they were safely behind the counter, Callidus and Amicus ran over to join them. The fortune seeker landed heavily on the floor next to Jake, his pistol flashing empty.

"Where's Amicus?" asked Jake, looking around.

The Altian was lying a few feet away, clutching his chest and writhing in pain.

"Blast it," wheezed Amicus, blood trickling through his fingers. "I must be getting slow."

"We've got to help him," said Jake.

"Yes, but how?" asked Callidus. "We're pinned down."

"We should surrender."

"I don't think they're looking for prisoners," whimpered Capio, cowering under a drinks tray.

"We have to try," said Jake.

Callidus nodded. It was pointless trying to take on so many troops.

"Hold your fire," he shouted, throwing his pistol over the counter. "We surrender."

The troopers either didn't notice or they didn't care. Their plasma rifles continued to rip into the thick wooden surface, blasting off great chunks. Kella screamed as a bottle exploded above her head and showered her in glass. It would only take a single palm grenade to finish them all.

"We're coming out," said Jake, standing up with his hands in the air.

To his astonishment the weapons fell silent.

Kella and Nanoo also surfaced from behind the counter, followed by Callidus and Capio. They walked toward the naval troops with their hands raised, stepping over broken furniture and shattered glass. Jake stopped to check on Amicus, but it was too late; the Altian general was dead.

"Hold it there," called out one of the troopers. "You're under arrest."

The interior of the ISS *Colossus* was the exact opposite of the *Dark Horse*. It was bright, spacious, and clean, with a working artificial-gravity system. There was no rust or wires hanging out of wall panels, and each member of the crew wore a smart, midnight-blue uniform. It was everything Jake had expected to find on a naval warship and he despised every detail. He had once craved a career in the Interstellar Navy, but not now that he knew what a bunch of cold-blooded killers they were.

Jake, Kella, Nanoo, Callidus, and Capio were handcuffed and marched through the ship to a holding cell, while Farid and Kodan were carted off to the medical bay.

The five of them remained in the holding cell for an hour, taking turns sitting on a narrow bench. Jake paced the floor, unable to rest. His mind was plagued with the questions that he should have asked Amicus, questions about Altus and his father, questions that may never get answered now. Jake had had so little time with him, but Amicus had been a connection to his past and proof that Altus existed.

"I'm hungry," complained Kella.

"You're always hungry," said Jake irritably.

"We wait long time," moaned Nanoo. "What happen next?"

"How should I know?" snapped Jake.

The cell door unlocked and slid open with an angry hiss. Two guards entered and stood to the side, making way for a man in an indigo uniform. He was accompanied by a woman in a designer suit with a large diamond brooch. The man looked old and sour, with pallid skin and white hair. A row of medals decorated his ornate jacket, and a long sword hung from his belt. His narrow dark eyes scanned the prisoners' faces, stopping when they reached Callidus.

"I know you," he said in a scratchy voice. "It's Captain Stone, isn't it?"

"Yes, sir." Callidus stood to attention. "It's been a long time, Admiral Nex."

"Captain Stone?" exclaimed Kella. "You work for the Interstellar Navy?"

"Not any more," said Callidus. "I used to be an officer in this fleet, but I left years ago to seek my fortune."

"Yes, what a pity," sneered Admiral Nex. "Did you ever find out what your head studs were for?"

"No."

"You had talent, Stone, and you could have gone far. But look at you now, a common fortune seeker, resisting arrest and opening fire on my troops."

"They fired first," said Jake angrily. "Your troops attacked the service port and killed our friend."

The admiral regarded Jake with a wry smile. "I've been looking for you, boy. It's good to finally meet you."

"Get away from me," warned Jake. "You're nothing but a liar and a murderer."

Admiral Nex glared at him with venomous eyes. "You don't know the half of it."

The woman cleared her throat.

"Is this the boy from Altus?" she asked, playing with her diamond brooch. "That's strange. His eyes didn't look that bright in the picture."

"My name is Jake," he said through gritted teeth. "Jake Cutler."

Jake could tell instantly that she was the richest person he had ever met. Her face sparkled with glittering makeup and her strawberry blonde hair had been molded to her scalp. The scent of expensive perfume filled the room, and her accent was pure first solar system. He wondered what she meant about his eyes. What picture?

"This is Commissioner Lamia Dolosa from the Galactic Trade Corporation," said Admiral Nex. "We would like to learn the location of Altus."

"It doesn't exist," claimed Callidus. "Altus is a myth. Everyone knows that."

"Nice try, Stone," said Admiral Nex. "I've spent my whole life searching for that planet. It's the only independent colony worth conquering. Altus is real all right and I'll execute anyone who says otherwise."

He grasped the hilt of his sword and waited for

any further outbursts. Commissioner Dolosa stepped forward to get a better look at Jake. Her nose twitched uneasily, as though their apparent poverty was contagious.

"Jake, you seem like a sweet child," she said, stooping down in her unnecessarily high heels. "Can you help us to find Altus? We know it has to be somewhere between Remota and that awful mafia spaceport, but we can't seem to find it. I promise we'll make it worth your while."

"Garbish," shouted Jake. "Amicus died protecting his home planet and I'll do the same."

Admiral Nex's face reddened.

"Insolent brat," he snarled. "We've not waited this long to fail now. You will help us, whether you like it or not. The next time we meet, you'll beg to tell me the location of Altus."

"Hey, leave him alone," said Kella.

"How dare you talk to me in that manner?" Admiral Nex was now scarlet with anger. "Guards, take them to the main prison level and prepare them for maximum interrogation. I'm tempted to send the lilac boy to our science team for dissection."

"You just try it." Jake stepped in front of Nanoo.

"Admiral, please," said Callidus. "You can't subject children to maximum interrogation."

"Do it now," roared the old man, shaking with rage. "I am Admiral Nex of the Interstellar Navy. Nobody tells me what to do."

Jake and the others were ushered out of the holding cell and taken to the main prison level, where the rooms were equipped for longer stays. Jake had no idea what maximum interrogation involved and he was in no hurry to find out.

Chapter 16

The Kalmar

Jake entered the new cell and discovered two familiar figures slumped on the bunks.

"Farid, Kodan, are you okay?"

"Hello, trouble," said Farid, holding his wounded head.

Both men were wrapped in bloodied bandages and looked as though they had been spat out by a space monster.

"You looking bad," said Nanoo.

"Thanks, kid." Farid attempted to sit up and failed. "The medics did a pretty good job of patching us up, but it still hurts like a case of Kalos scurvy."

Kodan groaned and rolled over to face the wall.

Jake handed Kella his pendant again, so she could relieve some of their pain and speed up their recovery. As she began to manipulate the crystals, Jake rounded on Callidus.

"Why didn't you tell us you were in the Interstellar Navy?"

"I'm not proud of it. I wasn't in my right mind when they signed me up for a six-year tour."

"That must have been one nasty hangover," said Farid.

Callidus nodded. "The first few years were the toughest and I'm ashamed of the orders I carried out. I've tried to forget that part of my life, but it haunts me every day. Now it feels strange to be aboard a naval warship, especially on this side of the cell door."

"That's karma for you," said Farid. "What goes around, comes around."

"Were you serving under Admiral Nex when my dad's ship was attacked?" Jake hated the idea of the fortune seeker working for the enemy.

"No, that was before my time," said Callidus. "I've been in many battles and I've destroyed lots of craft, but never an Altian ship."

"So what now?" asked Jake. "Are they really going to torture us?"

"It looks that way," said Callidus. "Unless you can tell them where to find Altus."

"They already know it's somewhere between Remota and Papa Don's spaceport," said Capio. "Which is more than we've found out. If the Interstellar Navy is unable to locate Altus with all of its resources and technology, what chance do we have?"

"We have Jake Cutler."

"I think you'll find that *we* don't have anything," corrected Kella. "The Interstellar Navy has the lot of us."

"I'm sorry, Cal," said Jake. "But I can't help you or anyone else to find Altus. I wish I knew the way home, so I could make my uncle Kear pay for what he has done, but the truth is, I have no idea."

His words lingered in the air like an unpleasant smell.

"It's okay," said Callidus. "Whatever happens, I have faith that you will somehow find your way home."

"Faith?" Jake was surprised to hear this word used by the fortune seeker. "I didn't know you were a religious man."

"We all have to believe in something."

The mighty warship engines rumbled to life, sending reverberations throughout the vessel.

"Where they take us?" asked Nanoo.

"A prison moon?" said Jake.

"I doubt it." Callidus climbed onto a bunk and closed his eyes. "If Commissioner Dolosa has her way, I expect we're setting course for somewhere between Remota and Papa Don's spaceport."

*   *   *

For three long hours Jake and the others remained in their prison cell, wondering whose name would be called out first to face maximum interrogation. It was impossible to concentrate on anything else, and Jake suspected that this was part of the torture.

Capio was particularly restless.

"We should make a deal with Admiral Nex and Commissioner Dolosa, before it's too late."

"What makes you think we could trust them?" said Callidus. "Not that we have anything to bargain with anyway, but if we did, I would rather make a pact with Kear Cutler."

"That was my next suggestion." Capio lowered his voice to a whisper. "There might be a bounty for the boy."

Jake couldn't believe what he was hearing.

"Capio," scolded Callidus. "Do you think for an instant that I would send a thirteen-year-old boy to his death, so we could collect his blood money?"

"Well, when you put it like that . . ."

Callidus tapped the side of his head with his finger.

"Use your minuscule brain for once in your life. I'm sure our reward for helping Jake to defeat Kear will be far greater than any bounty for his death."

"Far greater?"

"More money than even you can imagine," claimed Callidus. "Wealth beyond your greediest of dreams."

"That's a lot of money," said Capio, smirking. "I hadn't thought of it that way."

"I'm right here, you know." Jake stood in front of them, waving his arms. "I can hear what you're saying. If anyone will decide the size of your reward, it will be me, okay?"

Capio stopped smiling.

"Greed futile," said Nanoo. "Novu value education above all things. Knowledge is wealth."

Capio snorted. "Tell that to the directors of the Galactic Trade Corporation."

"Is that why you want to find Altus, Cal?" asked Jake. "Are you going to sell out my home planet to make your fortune?"

Callidus didn't answer.

"Why not?" said Capio, on his behalf. "Don't get me wrong, a reward would be nice, but why stop there? If we don't mine those crystal moons, someone else will. It might as well be us, right?"

"Why does it have to be anyone?" Jake felt betrayed. "No wonder Amicus was prepared to die for Altus, with greedy people like you trying to destroy it."

"Now wait a minute," said Callidus. "Let's not start fighting each other. We have to focus on escaping and getting Jake home."

"What about your reward?" asked Kella.

"Yes, of course I want a reward," said Callidus irritably. "I'm a fortune seeker and that's how I make a living. It doesn't mean that I'm prepared to commit genocide to fill my pockets. I'm not a blasted space pirate—no offense, Farid and Kodan."

"None taken." Farid laughed. "I can't speak for the rest of the crew, but I would sell my own grandmother for a crate of jewels. Would any of us destroy a whole planet out of greed? Nobody can say for sure, until they see those big old crystal moons for themselves."

Callidus turned to Jake, as serious as a cybermonk.

"Jake, I've always been fascinated by your planet, as long as I can remember, but it's not just about the treasure or the size of the reward. Trust me, there are easier ways to make money."

"So why do you want to find Altus?"

"I'm drawn to its mystery. I want to find the world that has eluded so many others for centuries. The Interstellar Navy took my decency. I need a sense of purpose, something that I can be proud of. Altus has always been the ultimate challenge, but now I want to find it for a different reason. You. If you let me, I'll take you home and help you to confront your uncle. I'm prepared to do whatever it takes to give Altus back its rightful ruler. Are you?"

Jake turned to Kella and Nanoo, who just shrugged. He didn't know if he could trust Callidus, but what if he couldn't find Altus without him? It was only a matter of time before the Interstellar Navy worked out its location. Jake had to get there first, by whatever means necessary.

"I'm going to trust you, Cal. I reckon you'll do the right thing when the time comes. Don't let me down."

"Thank you." Callidus put a hand on Jake's shoulder. "Your confidence in me means a lot."

For a moment they stared at each other, connected by a feeling of mutual respect that filled Jake with hope. It lasted for only a second, when someone cleared his throat. Admiral Nex stood in the doorway, accompanied by two men in red laboratory coats and black leather gloves. It was time for maximum interrogation.

"This is your last chance, boy," said Admiral Nex, his eyes fixed on Jake.

"Please be reasonable," protested Callidus.

"There's no need for such extremes. None of us knows the location of Altus."

"Back off, Stone," warned Admiral Nex. "My interrogators will find out if you're hiding anything."

"Take me," said Jake, stepping forward. "You'll see that we're telling the truth. No one else needs to suffer."

This act of courage seemed to amuse Admiral Nex.

"My boy," he said, "I applaud your bravery and it's a tempting offer, but I've already chosen someone to go first."

Two guards entered the cell and grabbed hold of Kella.

"Hey," she cried. "Get your hands off me."

"Let her go," demanded Jake, but he was pushed back by the men in red coats. "Kella hasn't done anything."

"Oh really?" sneered Admiral Nex. "Anyone who travels with space pirates is far from innocent. Unless you can tell me where to find Altus, we'll be forced to use our most severe methods of interrogation on her."

He signaled to the guards, who started to drag Kella away.

"Jake?" she said, her eyes filling with fear. "Help me."

Jake had never felt so powerless. He didn't have the information Admiral Nex wanted and he couldn't fight a warship full of naval troops. Kella Anderson was at the mercy of a merciless man.

"Well, boy?" asked Admiral Nex.

Jake opened his mouth to speak, but nothing came out. What could he say?

"Nothing?" Admiral Nex tutted and shook his head. "Oh, dear, that is a shame."

"Jake, do something!" screamed Kella.

And then it happened.

The ISS *Colossus* was hit with such force the impact sent shockwaves throughout the entire ship, knocking everyone to the floor. This was followed by a haunting sound of metal buckling under pressure.

"What was that?" Admiral Nex clambered to his feet.

"What you do, Jake?" asked Nanoo, with a mixture of fear and admiration.

"I didn't do anything," said Jake. "It wasn't me, I swear."

"Perhaps it was another craft," suggested Capio. "But who would be mad enough to take on the Interstellar Navy?"

Callidus shook his head. "That didn't sound like another ship."

"What else could it be?" asked Farid.

Further tremors shook the ISS *Colossus*, followed by the sound of laser cannon. In the cell, the lights dimmed to red and a siren sounded. Admiral Nex steadied himself and fumbled for his communicator.

"What's going on?" he barked into the device. "A what? Are you serious? How big?"

In the corridor outside, the two guards held on to Kella while awaiting further instructions.

"How should I know?" shouted Admiral Nex. "Are we too close for torpedoes? In that case, keep firing the cannon until I think of something."

Another shockwave rocked the ship.

Admiral Nex turned off his communicator. "It looks as though your interrogation will have to wait."

"How large is the kalmar?" asked Callidus, surprising everyone with the question.

"According to my first mate, it's the biggest space monster he's seen in years," said Admiral Nex. "It came out of an asteroid field as we passed and seized our hull. The laser cannon are struggling to penetrate its hide and we're too close for torpedoes. So, unless you have any bright ideas, I'm going to see if I can save my ship before it's torn apart."

"Actually," said Callidus. "I might be able to help."

"Might?" snapped Admiral Nex. "What do you mean might?"

"I know a way to destroy the beast," claimed Callidus. "But it will cost you."

"Don't be an idiot, Stone. We're talking about a ruddy kalmar. If this ship is destroyed we'll all die, so if you know a way to stop it, speak now and save your own neck."

"What's the point? If we survive this attack, my friends and I will be facing torture and death anyway. At least this way I get to take you down with me."

"Cal, what are you doing?" hissed Capio. "Have you lost your mind?"

"You're bluffing," said Admiral Nex, his eyes narrowing. "You don't know anything."

"Fine, have it your way." Callidus folded his arms. "Let me know how you get on with your new pet."

"Blast it, Stone, you always were stubborn. What's your price?"

"Let Jake and the others go, and I'll get rid of the kalmar."

"No deal."

"Those are my terms," said Callidus firmly. "You're going to lose Jake either way."

Admiral Nex turned scarlet again. He was being held ransom by a giant space squid and an ex-officer.

It was clearly too much for him to bear. He stormed out of the cell, sealing the door behind him.

"I hope you know what you're doing, Cal," said Capio.

"How did you know it was a kalmar?" asked Jake.

"It was only a guess," said Callidus. "The impact didn't feel like another ship or a stray asteroid."

Jake had read about space monsters in his storybooks, but he had assumed they were made up to frighten children. In his mind, he recalled an illustration of a giant squid-like creature chasing a passenger ship, with four glowing red eyes and long green tentacles.

"Do you really know how to kill a kalmar?" Farid sounded impressed.

"Yes. I once met someone who tried to catch one," said Callidus. "He never succeeded, but he did discover a weakness."

The attack grew more aggressive. It was only a matter of time before the warship hull was breached.

"Why laser cannon have no effect?" asked Nanoo.

"Kalmars have incredibly tough skin, so they can survive in space," explained Callidus. "Laser cannon only scratch the surface."

"Amazing," said Nanoo. "I never hear of such a creature. I hope we get to study it."

"Study it?" Capio pointed at the hull. "That overgrown star squid is trying to eat the lot of us and you want to study it?"

The cell door opened and Admiral Nex entered with four armed guards.

"You win, Stone. We can't shake the kalmar and the hull is starting to fracture. I don't know how much longer we can hold out, so you had better act fast."

"And the others?" asked Callidus.

"Yes, yes, they can go. I have a shuttle waiting on the hangar deck. Just hurry up and get that wretched thing off my ship."

"Okay," said Callidus. "I'll need all the frozen fish and high explosives you have on board."

Admiral Nex scowled. "What are you playing at?"

"Don't worry," said Callidus. "I won't harm your precious warship."

"You had better not." Admiral Nex dispatched two of his guards to fetch the supplies. "I want to be dining on kalmar steak tonight and not the other way around."

The lives of the entire crew now rested in the hands of a fortune seeker. Jake hoped that Callidus knew what he was doing. The warship shook with one of the biggest tremors yet, sending everyone flying. Jake peeled himself off the floor and rubbed his jaw. He was starting to dislike artificial gravity.

"Right, everyone to the hangar deck," instructed Callidus. "I'll be watching you on a display screen to make sure Admiral Nex keeps his word. Jake, assist Farid. Kella and Nanoo, support Kodan. Capio, I need you to stay here and help me."

"Why me?" whined Capio. "What can I do?"

"Trust me," said Callidus. "I'll make you a hero."

Jake paused by the door. "Cal, are you—"

"It's the only way," insisted the fortune seeker. "Now get moving. I've got a monster to kill."

Chapter 17

The Truth

The hangar deck on the ISS *Colossus* was big enough to hold thirty cargo haulers. Most of the craft docked there were fighters or shuttles lined up in neat rows, except for those dislodged by the kalmar attack. Jake wondered why Admiral Nex hadn't launched the fighters against the space monster, but then he figured their weapons would be even less effective than the enormous laser cannon.

Armed guards escorted him and the others to a small shuttle near the launch locks. Jake had read about these giant gateways, but he had never seen one up close. Launch locks were similar to air locks, only much larger. Most warships had two of them, or sometimes four, each of which could hold ten fighters at a time. The ISS *Colossus* had eight.

As they reached the shuttle, Jake noticed another vessel docked nearby, a craft that didn't belong on a naval warship.

"Hey," he said, almost letting go of Farid. "I've seen that ship before. It was on Remota the night we escaped."

There was no mistaking the distinctive black-and-white emblem painted on the side. It was the space pirate assault craft from Temple Hill. A mixture of fear and anger stirred inside Jake. He glared at the white skull in a space helmet, wanting to punch its stupid fixed grin.

"What's that doing here?" wondered Kella.

"Navy capture it?" suggested Nanoo.

"But it's not damaged," said Jake, examining the craft. "That's strange, the shape of the cockpit and the angle of its windows are the same as a naval shuttle."

"Jake, we don't have time for this," pressed Kella.

"Don't you see?" he said. "The assault craft *is* a naval shuttle. It wasn't space pirates who attacked the monastery on Remota, but the Interstellar Navy."

"Jake—"

"Think about it; their pirate outfits are brand new and their weapons are naval standard. They have to be troops in disguise. The Interstellar Navy has no authority on independent colonies, so they had to fake a raid to avoid causing a major incident."

"He's right, you know," said Farid, leaning on

Jake's shoulder. "I've never seen a pirate craft that spotless."

The hangar deck shook violently.

"Keep moving," ordered one of the guards, pushing them with his rifle.

Jake took a final look at the assault craft and helped Farid up the steps of the waiting shuttle. He knew that Callidus would be waiting until they were clear.

Once inside, they closed the shuttle door and strapped themselves in, ready for takeoff, when something dawned on Kella.

"Who's going to operate this thing?"

Jake looked around the cabin. Farid and Kodan were injured, and he doubted Kella or Nanoo had ever flown a shuttle.

"I'll do it," he said.

"You?"

"I know more about ships than most pilots," he boasted. "I've done loads of online simulations, and I've even had lessons in a security shuttle."

"Thanks for the offer, kid," said Farid. "But I'll take the helm."

"Are you sure?" Jake felt a mixture of relief and disappointment.

Farid shrugged. "There's only one way to find out."

The first mate climbed into the cockpit and flipped several switches, but his movements were slow and rigid. He released the brake and the shuttle jerked forward, trundling across the hangar deck toward the launch locks.

"Look out!" cried Jake, spotting the fake assault craft sliding toward them.

Farid attempted to swerve, but his reactions were not fast enough. The assault craft slammed into the side of the shuttle, sending it crashing into a row of fighters. Jake's straps cut into his chest as the shuttle buried itself under a heap of midnight blue metal. He fell back in his seat, waiting for the world to stop moving and his chest to stop hurting.

Kella and Nanoo moaned in pain. In the cockpit something beeped. The engine was still running, so why had they stopped? Then he noticed Farid's arm hanging limply through the door.

Jake released his straps and rushed to the cockpit. Farid had collapsed over the controls and was out cold. Now there was no choice; Jake had to fly the shuttle.

"What's going on?" asked Kella. "What are you doing up there?"

"Getting us out of here!" Jake strapped himself into the copilot's seat and seized the controls.

The instruments were standard design, making them easy to recognize. Jake punched a few buttons and squeezed the throttle. The shuttle responded and rolled backward, but there was a horrific scraping sound as it wrenched free from the tangled mass of fighter craft.

"This isn't as easy as it looks."

Jake crunched the gears and steered the wobbling shuttle toward the launch locks, slowly gathering speed. He saw another row of fighters sliding into his path and accelerated hard, but clipped the last craft. The hangar deck swirled past the windows as the shuttle was sent spinning into an open launch lock. Jake slammed on the brakes and brought the shuttle to an abrupt halt inches from the lock wall.

Huge inner doors closed behind them, sealing the shuttle inside the launch lock, before the outer doors parted like an iron curtain to reveal an ocean of stars.

"Hello, big black," said Jake, shaking with adrenaline. "It's good to see you again."

He leaned on the throttle and the shuttle charged forward, pinning him to his seat. It reached the edge of the lock and burst into space.

"What's going on?" mumbled Farid, sitting up. "Where are we?"

"We've escaped," said Jake, his knuckles white from squeezing the controls. "Are you all right?"

"I must have hit my head, but I'll be okay."

Jake switched the shuttle to autopilot and returned to the cabin to check on the others. His eyes were instantly drawn to the scene outside the rear window. The kalmar was wrapped around the ISS *Colossus* in a deadly embrace, two giants of space fighting for survival. Bursts of laser bolts sparkled like fireworks, while huge tentacles smashed and crushed the metal hull.

What was Callidus waiting for? Why hadn't he destroyed the beast? A worrying thought crossed Jake's mind. What if there was no plan? What if Callidus had lied to save him and the others? What if the fortune seeker had no idea how to kill a kalmar?

Jake cursed himself for leaving without Callidus and Capio. Between the Interstellar Navy and the space monster, the two men didn't stand a chance. Why hadn't he insisted that they be released as well?

None of this would have happened if Jake had grown up on Altus, where he belonged. It was all his uncle's fault. Anger swelled inside him as he thought about his father, the cyber-monks, Amicus Kent,

Callidus and Capio. Jake watched the ISS *Colossus* shrink into the distance and vowed to make Kear Cutler pay, whatever it took.

"What that was?" asked Nanoo.

"What what was?" said Jake. "I mean, what was what?"

"Shuttle tremor like a quack."

"I think you mean quake," corrected Kella.

"In space?" Jake found this hard to believe.

"I felt it as well," said Kella. "It was like something nudging the hull."

"Perhaps warship explode." Nanoo flung open his arms to demonstrate.

"With Callidus and Capio inside?" Jake had been worrying about the two men since they had lost sight of the ISS *Colossus*. "We should go back. They might need our help."

"Go back?" said Kella. "What if Nanoo is right and the naval warship has been destroyed? We would be alone with a giant kalmar."

Jake knew she was right, but if it hadn't been for Callidus and Capio, they would still be prisoners aboard the naval warship. He pictured the two men floating in space, injured and unconscious, while the giant kalmar gobbled up naval troops around them.

"If we not go back," said Nanoo, "why we turn around?"

Jake checked the window and saw the stars circling by outside.

"Hey, Farid," he shouted. "What's going on?"

"We're heading back to the warship."

"Why?"

"We have no choice." Farid stuck his head through the cockpit door. "We're almost out of fuel and there are no planets or spaceports nearby. It looks as though Admiral Nex didn't want us to go far."

"But we had a deal," said Jake indignantly.

"I knew we couldn't trust that sneaky two-faced wretch!" Kella fumed.

Farid steered the shuttle back to the coordinates where they had left the ISS *Colossus*. When they arrived, he turned off the thrusters and let the shuttle drift.

"Are we here?" asked Jake, joining him in the cockpit.

"Yep."

"So where are they?"

Farid shrugged. "No idea."

Jake scanned the section of space where he had expected to see the kalmar still wrapped around the naval warship, but there was nothing.

"I don't understand. Where have they gone?"

Farid sat forward and pointed. "What's that?"

Jake caught sight of two objects floating in the distance, which he could have sworn were people.

"Are they waving at us?"

"Let's find out."

Farid gave the throttle a squeeze and the shuttle moved closer. Jake could now clearly see two men in naval space suits.

"I don't believe it." Farid slapped the dashboard. "It's Callidus and Capio."

"What?" exclaimed Jake. "But how?"

It seemed impossible that the two men could have survived the kalmar attack and escaped the ISS *Colossus*, but there they were. As the shuttle pulled up next to them, Callidus and Capio grabbed hold of its sidebars.

Farid tuned into their helmet communicators. "Hello, friends. What happened to the kalmar?"

"We killed it," said Callidus, pulling himself up to the cockpit window. "Can you let us in?"

Farid shifted uncomfortably in his seat. "I'm afraid that's not possible."

"Why not?"

"There's no air lock and we don't have space suits," said Farid. "I can't open the door without suffocating everyone inside."

"I knew it was too good to be true." Capio kicked the side of the shuttle.

"We're not done yet," said Callidus. "We can hang on to the sidebars, while Farid tows us to safety. It'll be okay, as long as he doesn't accelerate too fast."

Farid shook his head. "There's nowhere nearby and we're almost out of fuel. I was hoping to salvage some supplies from the warship wreckage."

"What happened to the ISS *Colossus*?" asked Jake. "How did you kill the kalmar?"

"I told you that I met someone who tried to catch one," said Callidus. "He used fish as bait and discovered that kalmars detest seafood."

"So what?" said Farid. "I don't like salad, but it wouldn't kill me."

"No, but high explosives would." Callidus smiled. "We set the timers and went down to the rear cargo hold. The kalmar was outside the doors with its mouth wide open."

"It was horrible," said Capio, shuddering inside his space suit. "The most revolting mouth I've ever seen. All that thick saliva, yuck . . . and that deafening screech . . . horrible."

"So what happened next?" asked Jake.

"We fed the kalmar a cocktail of frozen fish and high explosives," said Callidus. "I opened the doors and Capio pushed the crates into the waiting mouth. A few moments later, the kalmar cried out and released the ship, thrashing and writhing as it tried to escape the taste. The explosives detonated and blew the beast into a thousand pieces, but it was still close enough for the blast to knock out the ship's electrics."

"You two disabled the ISS *Colossus*?" laughed Farid.

"Not intentionally," said Callidus. "But it presented us with an opportunity to escape."

"A leap of faith, he called it," snorted Capio. "'Have you ever taken a leap of faith?' 'What's that?' I say. 'It's when you enter a situation without knowing how it's going to end,' he says. 'No,' I say, 'my mother doesn't approve of gambling.' 'Well, it's a good thing she's not here,' he says, and drags me out of the cargo doors."

"You jumped into open space?" said Farid. "Are you mad?"

Callidus shrugged. "It seemed like a good idea at the time."

"Where's the warship now?" asked Jake.

"It's somewhere over there." Callidus pointed toward a patch of space. "You'll struggle to find it with its lights out."

"So where do we go from here?" asked Farid.

No one spoke.

"There must be something we can do," said Callidus. "We can't just wait here until our oxygen runs out."

"We could activate the distress beacon," suggested Jake. "And hope a passing ship picks up the signal."

"How do we know another naval warship won't hear it?" asked Farid.

"That's a gamble we might have to take," said Callidus.

Capio glanced over his shoulder and let out a whimper.

"Don't look now," he groaned. "But the ISS *Colossus* has regained power."

Chapter 18

The Rescue

Jake spotted the naval warship in the distance, partially lit and turning slowly toward them. Its mighty laser cannon were prepped for battle and its launch locks were wide open, releasing a swarm of fighter craft. He knew they were about to feel the might of the Interstellar Navy.

"I'm sorry, Jake," said Callidus, placing his glove on the cockpit window. "We almost made it."

Farid thumped the dashboard in frustration. Jake knew it wasn't in a Space Dog's nature to give up without a fight, but what other choice did they have? The first mate leaned forward and let his hand hover over the communicator, waiting until the last second to contact the Interstellar Navy.

Jake stared at the cloud of approaching fighters, desperately trying to think of a way to escape, when the communicator crackled to life.

"Ahoy there, naval shuttle," croaked an unmistakable voice. "What are you lazy layabouts doing out here? I'm missing a first mate, a master-at-arms, and some pesky passengers."

A wide grin spread across Farid's face.

"Ahoy there, Captain," he said. "It's nice of you to join us."

"Yeah, yeah, save the mushy stuff. We're coming up fast behind you, so brace yourselves for a rapid rescue."

Jake spotted the *Dark Horse* on the scanner. Granny Leatherhead wasn't exaggerating, the cargo hauler was approaching at top speed. He quickly warned the others to hold on to something.

"Where did they come from?" asked Kella, strapping herself in.

"They must have been following us," said Jake. "Waiting for the right moment."

"What are they going to do?" Kella peered out of the window. "Their loading ramp is wide open. Can this shuttle fit inside their cargo hold?"

"Not easy," said Nanoo. "Pilot require great skill not to crash at fast speed. What you reckon, Jake?"

"I don't know, but we're about to find out."

Callidus and Capio flattened themselves against the shuttle as the *Dark Horse* approached. Jake knew they had just moments before the naval warship and fighters opened fire. He could still hear Granny

Leatherhead's voice booming through the communicator.

"Hoist the flag and show 'em our colors, boys," she ordered the crew. "Activate the shields, roll out the big guns, and fire!"

Jake watched as a protective force field coated the ship, shimmering like a layer of crumpled green glass. Underneath it, camouflaged panels lifted to reveal space pirate markings, while hidden gun ports slid open to uncover a row of sawed-off laser cannon. The *Dark Horse* fired at the fighters, forcing the naval pilots to break formation and scatter among the stars. The cargo hauler swooped down on the stranded shuttle, scooping up the small craft into its belly.

"Good work, Nichelle," croaked Granny Leatherhead. "Now bring her about hard. We need to get our cross-boned butts out of here before someone scuttles us."

"Aye, Captain."

A laser bolt caught the side of the *Dark Horse*, knocking it sideways. Nichelle took evasive action, steering first one way and then cutting to the other.

"Full speed ahead," barked Granny Leatherhead. "Let's put some stars between us and that warship."

Nichelle opened the throttle to maximum, but it wasn't necessary. The ISS *Colossus* broke off its pursuit and recalled its fighter craft. The warship needed to stop for repairs, after taking damage from both the kalmar attack and the explosion.

The *Dark Horse* had escaped for now, but Admiral Nex would never give up. He would search every known planet and spaceport until he had hunted down the Space Dogs. Now that they had been identified, there would be nowhere safe for Jake and the others to hide from the Interstellar Navy.

A few hours later, both crew and guests were summoned to the dining area on the first deck. They crammed into the room, sitting or standing wherever there was space. Farid and Kodan were strapped into chairs and wrapped in blankets. Jake sat between Callidus and Kella, waiting for the captain, wondering what she wanted. He had already told her about Baden Scott and Amicus Kent.

"Cal."

"Yes, Jake."

"I've been meaning to ask about the metal studs in your head. What are they?"

"I wish I knew," said Callidus. "I've had them for as long as I can recall, but then I don't remember much before the Interstellar Navy. I was in a bad way back then."

"Maybe you were a cyber-monk. The brothers on Remota had skull implants, so they could connect better with technology."

"Me? A cyber-monk?" Callidus laughed at this idea. "Brother Stone? It's possible, but not very likely. I prefer to write my own moral code."

"It's funny not knowing your past, isn't it," said Jake. "I didn't know that I was the rightful ruler of Altus until Amicus came along. Mind you, there's still a part of me that wishes I didn't know, because life used to be a lot simpler."

"At least it's given you a purpose," said Callidus. "I'm not sure what I'll do once we find Altus."

Granny Leatherhead stomped into the room. Her faded combat suit was held together by a collection of clips, straps, and patches, which covered most of the fabric. In one hand, she clutched a battered silver skull-shaped helmet, and in the other, a bulky laser pistol. Her long leather coat hung from her shoulders, like the cloak of a military commander.

"Good news, folks," she said, climbing onto a table. "It looks as though we've shaken off the Interstellar Navy."

Everyone cheered and banged the tables in celebration.

"Nobody m-m-messes with the Space Dogs," stammered Woorak.

"I thought that would please you, but let's not get carried away. It won't be long before they catch up with us and we might not be so lucky next time. Admiral Nex is a nasty piece of work and I have no desire to feel the wrath of his laser cannon, so I've called you all here to agree on what we're going to do about it."

"All of us?" said Callidus.

"Aye, everyone." Granny Leatherhead's gray eye scanned the room to see if anyone dared to object. "All of our lives are in danger, so it's only right that we work together to sort out this mess. From now on, guests will no longer be confined to their quarters. Instead, they'll be treated as part of the crew. Is that clear?"

"Aye," said everyone except Kella.

"And the same goes for special cargo," added Granny Leatherhead, blinking.

"Is she trying to wink at me?" whispered Kella.

"I think so," said Jake. "It's difficult to tell with that eye patch, but let's assume it's a good thing."

Kella nodded and smiled.

Jake was thrilled to become an official space-jacker. He glanced across to Scargus and Manik, who gave him a proud thumbs-up.

"Okay, what are our options?" asked Callidus.

"We can run, hide, or fight," said Granny Leatherhead. "Personally, I don't mind running and hiding, but I'm not sure I want to do it for the rest of my life."

"If we stand and fight, do we have any assets?" asked Callidus. "You know, like powerful allies or secret weapons?"

"No, not really." Nichelle chewed her thumbnail. "We don't tend to mix with other crews and our biggest advantage has always been surprise, but now our cover has been blown."

"We've got six sawed-off laser cannon and a resourceful crew," said Scargus. "That must count for something."

"What about Admiral Nex?" asked Manik. "Callidus, you know him. Does he have any weaknesses?"

"I know he's a cruel man who will stop at nothing to get what he wants," said Callidus. "He's obsessed with power and glory. Altus would be his ultimate trophy, immortalizing him in history."

"What about you all?" asked Granny Leatherhead, turning to Jake, Kella, and Nanoo. "What can you do?"

"Well, I'm the rightful ruler of Altus," said Jake. "Kella is a talented healer and Nanoo knows about Novu technology."

"Novu technology, eh?" she mused. "Tell me, captain castaway, can you help us?"

"Me?" Nanoo was caught off guard. "I not sure. Perhaps I can increase laser cannon power and make ship defenses strong."

"Is fighting really our best option?" asked Kella.

"No," said Jake. "It's not."

Granny Leatherhead stepped down from the table. "What's brewing in your brain, Kid Cutler?"

Jake liked having a pirate nickname.

"There are probably thousands of naval troops searching for the *Dark Horse*. If we try to fight, we'll be captured or killed. We should make a run for it."

"Run where?" asked Nichelle. "Not even the independent colonies are safe now."

"Altus," said Jake. "If we find Altus, it will be the ultimate hideout, because nobody knows its location. Commissioner Dolosa reckons it's somewhere between Remota and Papa Don's spaceport, which is nearby."

"Altus?" croaked Granny Leatherhead.

"Jake has a point," said Callidus. "Admiral Nex wouldn't expect us to return there so soon. It would give us time to explore the area."

"What if we don't find it?" argued Granny Leatherhead. "We've not had much luck so far. If our search failed, we would be stuck in the open with nowhere to hide."

"That's true," said Callidus. "But would we be any worse off than we are now?"

Granny Leatherhead tapped her nails on her space helmet while she considered the idea. It had been their intention to look for Altus, so Jake's suggestion wasn't completely crazy.

"What about Kear Cutler?" asked Capio. "Don't get me wrong, nobody wants to locate Altus more than I do, but even if we find it, Jake's uncle won't be pleased to see us."

"The coward has a point," said Granny Leatherhead. "If Jake is serious about taking his place as the rightful ruler, we would have to fight for it. I've never spacejacked a planet before, surface raids are usually too dangerous."

"It's a risk," Callidus agreed. "But I would rather take my chances on Altus than battle the entire Interstellar Navy."

"We might not have to fight anyone," said Kella, "if the Altian people accept Jake as their rightful ruler."

"Okay, okay, I've heard enough." Granny Leatherhead waved her laser pistol in the air. "We need to make a decision. All those in favor of searching for Altus, hold up your hands."

Callidus and Jake lifted their arms, followed by Kella and Nanoo. The crew swapped uncertain looks, before slowly showing their support, until only Capio was left.

"If we must," he groaned, raising his hand.

"It's unanimous," said Granny Leatherhead. "We'll set course for Papa Don's."

The room cleared and everyone returned to their quarters. It would be a few days before they reached the illegal spaceport, but then what? The entire plan depended on Jake's finding Altus. He was now under serious pressure to work out its location ... and he had no idea how.

Chapter 19

The Death Trap

Over the next couple of days, Jake spent his time either practicing with the cutlass or researching Altian legends. He still didn't feel ready for the challenges ahead, but who would? If they somehow evaded the Interstellar Navy, located Altus, and defeated his uncle, would he really be expected to rule an entire planet?

Nanoo and Manik spent their days building gadgets out of spare parts. So far, they had created a lie detector that was accurate within two yards, a personal force field generator that could be clipped to a belt, and an X-ray device that was able to see through most known materials. Jake admired Nanoo's technical skills, but he couldn't see how these gadgets would help them to find Altus.

Kella accepted the role of ship's medic and devoted her time to cleaning up the medical bay. Apart from crystal healing and basic first aid, she had no medical training, and so she used Jake's handheld computer to teach herself more.

"If I become the ruler of Altus, I'll help you to find Jeyne," vowed Jake over dinner. "And get you back to Taan-Centaur, Nanoo."

"Promise?" said Kella, chomping on a freeze-dried biscuit.

"Promise."

"How you get me home?" asked Nanoo, slipping food into a neck slit. "Taan-Centaur is far away. My spaceship had superior engine for intergalactic exploration. Your ships need to travel for many years without stop and *Dark Horse* not carry enough supplies. It sad, but I not see my people again."

"Don't give up hope," said Kella, putting an arm around him. "We'll find a way."

Jake nodded. "We could build a Novu engine that is powerful enough to make the trip."

"It possible," said Nanoo. "Not easy, but challenge is good."

"If anyone can do it, you can." But Jake knew his words meant nothing if they failed to locate Altus.

"Do you know something?" Kella flashed him a smile. "You independent colonists aren't so bad after all."

"Ha," said Jake. "And I suppose not everyone from the United Worlds is stuck-up."

Kella poked out her tongue.

"Hey," said Nanoo, pointing at the porthole window. "We pass asteroid field."

Jake looked through the scratched glass. "I've never seen so many in one place."

He watched the lifeless boulders float past the ship like a sea of stone. It made him think about the asteroid field that had claimed his father. He tried to picture someone in a space suit drifting helplessly out of sight.

"Hey, there something in asteroid field," said Nanoo. "It look like kalmar family."

Jake scanned the rocky mass and spotted movement. Nanoo was right, there was an adult kalmar with two young. How could anything live in such a dangerous place? Jake watched the little ones playing among the asteroids, as though they had no cares in the universe. It was difficult to imagine such innocent-looking creatures growing up and attacking huge spaceships.

"In the stories, kalmars spin webs between asteroids to catch food," said Jake. "But what could they possibly eat out here, apart from space barnacles?"

"People," groaned Kella, recalling their last encounter.

"Well, it good that kalmar not see us," said Nanoo.

Jake mulled something over in his mind.

"If kalmars can live in asteroid fields, do you reckon other things could survive in them?"

Kella raised an eyebrow. "You mean like your father?"

"Yes," he admitted.

"I suppose it's possible," she said. "But kalmar hide is a lot thicker than skin and your father would have had to avoid being crushed by a thousand asteroids. I've never heard of anyone beating those kind of odds."

Jake's heart sank, but he refused to give up hope. If anyone could survive an asteroid field, it had to be his father.

Nanoo finished eating and returned to the engine room to work on the shield generators, while Jake and Kella kept an eye on the space monsters. When they were clear of the asteroid field, Kella noticed something else through the porthole window.

"That's strange," she said. "There's a gap in the stars."

"What do you mean?" asked Jake.

Kella drew on the glass with her finger. "There are thousands of stars in this constellation except for one section that doesn't contain any."

"You're right." Jake squinted at the window. "It's a perfect black circle in a cluster of white lights. What is that?"

"A planet," said Kella. "It must be a giant planet blocking out the stars."

Jake dared to hope. "Altus?"

"What in the name of Zerost is going on?" demanded Granny Leatherhead, storming onto the bridge in a floral nightgown and gravity boots. "Which one of you blasted blowhorns woke me up with your shouting?"

"I'm sorry, Captain," said Jake. "But Kella has spotted a gap in the stars and we think it might be Altus."

"I should have guessed you two had something to do with it," she croaked, rubbing her tired eye with her fist.

"That patch of space does look strange," said Farid, pointing at his computer display.

The first mate was joined by Callidus, Capio, and Nichelle, who all nodded in agreement.

"Altus, eh? Just like that?" Granny Leatherhead tied back her straggly silver hair and studied the image on the display screen. "I suppose there's only one way to find out. Nichelle, move us closer to that thing."

"Aye, Captain."

The *Dark Horse* made its way to the gap in the stars, which ended up being a lot larger than Jake had anticipated.

"That's odd," said Nichelle, blowing a strand of blue hair out of her eyes. "I can feel the ship being pulled toward the gap and it's getting stronger."

"It's not just the ship." Farid checked his scanners. "A few of the stars have moved as well."

"What are you talking about?" snapped Granny Leatherhead. "I've never heard of anything that powerful, especially not some big black gap."

"No, not a gap," corrected Callidus with alarm. "It's a hole, a black hole!"

The *Dark Horse* was heading straight for a black hole, an invisible hazard feared by all space-faring crews. Few craft encountered one and survived to tell the tale.

"Callidus is right," said Farid. "How did we not recognize the signs? Look at the way the light bends around it."

"That's called gravitational lensing," said Jake, showing off his knowledge. "A black hole is created when a star collapses, but it's more of a sphere than a hole, spinning so fast that it creates a sort of super-gravity. The reason it looks flat is because you can't see any light reflecting off—"

"Let's save the science lesson," interrupted Granny Leatherhead, "because right now I would like to change course away from that thing. Nichelle, turn this ship around."

"Aye, Captain."

Nichelle tugged at the controls, but nothing happened.

"Well?" asked Granny Leatherhead impatiently. "I said turn her around."

"I'm trying," Nichelle insisted, switching to full throttle. "We're caught in the gravitational pull."

Jake tried to watch the rotating black void on the computer display, but he could see only cold, dark emptiness, as though he were staring at death itself. It made him feel small and helpless.

"What's in there?" asked Kella. "Where does everything go?"

"Nobody knows," said Jake. "Nothing can escape a black hole, not even light. If we get sucked inside it, we'll never be seen again."

The *Dark Horse* vibrated as Nichelle fought to change direction.

"Come on," she said, heaving at the controls. "Turn, you stubborn old turkey!"

"Keep it up," said Granny Leatherhead. "We're getting too close to that unholy hole for my liking."

The *Dark Horse* shook violently and red lights

flashed on the various displays. It reminded Jake of the kalmar attack a few days before, only there wasn't a giant squid-like monster outside, but something much larger and far more dangerous. Nichelle threw her full weight behind the controls and the ship responded, turning in a wide arc away from the black hole.

"We're almost clear," she said, puffing, her cheeks flushed.

"Good," said Farid. "Because we've got company."

The crew gathered around his scanner.

"Who is it?" asked Granny Leatherhead.

"Another ship," he said. "No, wait, there are two of them."

"Interstellar Navy?"

"Too small. I don't think they're commercial vessels either, judging by their speed."

"The space mafia?" suggested Jake.

"Perhaps," said Farid, looking up the ships on the stellar-net.

There was something wrong. Jake didn't know what it was or why he felt so anxious, but there was something making him nervous. He chewed his lip as he waited for Farid to speak.

"Crystal hunters," reported the first mate. "Those ships are registered to crystal hunters, by the names of Kain Stabbard and Jala Jenkins."

Jake bit his lip so hard that he drew blood. "It's the people who stopped me in Papa Don's spaceport."

"Those creepy cretins," said Granny Leatherhead. "What do they want?"

"The same thing as everyone else." Jake placed a protective hand over his pendant.

"Are they dangerous?" she asked.

"It's difficult to tell," said Farid. "There are only two ships, but they are fast and probably armed."

Granny Leatherhead examined the metallic shapes on the computer display.

"Hmm, I've dealt with worse than those dunderheads, but let's play it safe and raise the shields."

"We can't," said Nichelle. "The shields have been taken down while Nanoo and Manik work on them."

"What use are stronger defenses after a battle?" growled Granny Leatherhead. "Tell those tech twins to get the shields back up immediately."

"Aye, Captain," said Nichelle. "But it might take them awhile, even with help from Scargus."

"Those incompetent idiots. What about the laser cannon? I'm assuming they weren't stupid enough to recalibrate those at the same time."

Nichelle's nervous expression suggested that Nanoo and Manik were indeed that stupid.

"I don't believe it!" screeched Granny Leatherhead, throwing her hands up in despair. "This is what I get for taking on passengers. How are we supposed to defend ourselves? Can we at least make a run for it, or have they dismantled the engine as well?"

"The engine's fine," said Nichelle. "But we're trapped between the crystal hunters, the black hole, and the asteroid field."

Granny Leatherhead screamed and paced the bridge. The crystal hunters' ships were closer now and Jake could make out their sharp features, like silver daggers flying through space. He recalled Kain in his mind, remembering how the rat-faced man seemed like a wild animal, with his black fur coat and tattooed claw marks.

The communicator crackled ominously.

"Ahoy, cargo hauler," said Kain, his husky voice seeping through the speakers.

Granny Leatherhead forced a smile. "Ahoy, crystal hunters. How can we help you?"

"We have unfinished business with the boy and his pendant," said Kain. "Hand him over and the rest of you can leave with your lives."

"What could you possibly want with my cabin boy?" she asked sweetly.

"Don't play innocent with me, old woman. We know his pendant is from Altus and I'm betting it can lead us there. If you don't send him over, we'll cut open your ship and take it."

The *Dark Horse* might have been defenseless, but Granny Leatherhead was in no mood to surrender.

"Nobody threatens the Space Dogs, especially not a cheap crystal collector like you."

Kain laughed maliciously.

"I never bluff," he said. "You have five minutes, before we turn your ship into stardust."

The communicator fell silent.

"We have to do something," said Callidus.

"Yes, but what?" asked Granny Leatherhead. "Throw insults?"

"Why don't we give them Jake?" suggested Capio. "Don't get me wrong, I like the lad, but is anyone worth dying for?"

Granny Leatherhead eyed Jake in the same way a starving family might regard their pet dog.

"There must be another way," said Callidus.

Jake knew there wasn't. He was the only one who could save the ship. His pendant was worth the lives of the crew, but did it really contain the secrets of Altus? The three stones represented the three crystal moons. What about the rest of the design? Did the gold symbolize the sands of Altus? Was the swirling border important? He stepped forward, his heart heavy and his mouth dry.

"I—" he began.

"Hold on," said Farid. "There's another craft on the scanner."

"More crystal hunters?" asked Granny Leatherhead.

"No, much bigger," said Farid. "It's the ISS *Colossus*."

Chapter 20

Battle of the Black Hole

The enormous warship drew alongside the crystal hunters. Its midnight-blue hull was scarred with tentacle marks and its lights were still flickering.

"What are they doing?" croaked Granny Leatherhead. "Farid, see if you can tap into the crystal hunters' communicators."

"Aye, Captain."

To begin with, there was only static while the first mate searched for the right frequency, but then Kain's husky voice rustled through the speakers once more.

". . . thank you for stopping by, but this is a private matter and none of your concern."

"I disagree." Jake recognized the sour tones of Admiral Nex. "The crew of this cargo hauler are wanted for crimes of space piracy. If nothing else, they've stolen a naval shuttle, which we've been tracking for days. You will depart this area immediately or face the consequences."

"I'm sorry, but we can't do that." Kain sounded furious. "They have something of mine and I'm not leaving without it."

"What a pity."

The communicators fell silent.

"What does that mean?" asked a female voice, which Jake recognized as Jala. "Kain, maybe we should—"

Without warning, the ISS *Colossus* attacked. Ten laser cannon fired on the crystal hunters' ships, their powerful beams eating through the electronic shields. Within seconds, one of the ships exploded. The other returned fire, but it barely touched the warship before its hull tore open.

"Did you see what they did to the crystal hunters?" whimpered Capio, the blood draining from his face.

"Good. That solves one of our problems," said Granny Leatherhead. "But it still leaves us trapped. Farid, how long before those moon goons are in firing range?"

"Less than a minute and closing."

"Blast it." Granny Leatherhead activated the ship's alarm and snatched up the intercom. "Battle stations, everyone! We're about to engage a super-destroyer, but without any shields or weapons.

This is about as bad as it gets. Make me proud, my Space Dogs."

"We're going to fight?" said Capio in disbelief. "This worthless old wreck against the most powerful warship in the Interstellar Navy? Are you insane?"

"What would you suggest we do, you curly-haired coward?" snapped Granny Leatherhead. "Stop complaining and do something useful, before I throw you into that black hole myself."

The ISS *Colossus* was bearing down on the *Dark Horse*, like a giant metal shark descending on a small rusty mollusk.

"What are your orders, Captain?" asked Nichelle, holding the ship steady.

"Turn her around."

"What did you say?"

"I said turn her around." Granny Leatherhead's eye narrowed. "We need to move closer to the black hole."

Nichelle twisted in her seat. "You want to get closer to that thing?"

"How many times do I have to say it? Yes, I want us to move closer to that death trap, because I'm hoping the Interstellar Navy won't be foolish enough to follow."

"And what if they do?" asked Callidus.

"Then we'll give them everything we've got, by Zerost!"

The *Dark Horse* turned back toward the black hole and allowed gravity to draw it nearer. Jake wondered how close they could get before it was too late to pull out.

"We're taking an incredible risk," protested Callidus. "How long do you propose staying here? The warship might not follow us, but it can wait out there for weeks, possibly months if necessary."

"At least that will buy us some time to come up with a plan," said Farid.

Nanoo entered the bridge. "What going on? Scargus say we trapped between black hole and navy warship."

"That about sums up our situation," said Granny Leatherhead. "Why aren't you downstairs fixing the shields?"

"We finish." Nanoo beamed with pride. "Thanks to Novu technology, our shields now five times stronger. We so tough, we could wrestle kalmar."

"Five times stronger, eh?" said Granny Leatherhead. "That's more like it! What about my laser cannon?"

"Fully operating," said Nanoo. "Cannon packing big punch."

Granny Leatherhead's single eye sparkled.

"So, you're not completely useless," she said, barely containing a crooked smile.

"Captain," interrupted Farid. "The ISS *Colossus* is contacting us."

Granny Leatherhead picked up the communicator, as though it were a dead rat.

"Ahoy, naval warship. What do you want, Nex?"

"Ahoy, indeed, pirate vessel," said the cold, venomous voice. "I want you to hand over the Cutler boy. Don't waste time trying to negotiate. You're trapped and you know it."

Granny Leatherhead glanced at Nanoo and smiled. "In your dreams, navy nut. You'll have to come and get us. I'd rather take my chances in the black hole than surrender to you."

"Pirate scum," snarled Admiral Nex. "It's taken me eleven years to track down that boy and his pendant, ever since I found his picture aboard an Altian shipwreck, but I would rather see him dead than let you escape again. Prepare to be boarded, you foul space hag."

The communicator fell silent.

"He's bluffing," assured Granny Leatherhead. "No naval officer would be that irresponsible."

"I wouldn't count on it," said Farid, tracking the

warship's movements. "The ISS *Colossus* has entered the gravity field of the black hole. It looks as though we'll get to try out those new defenses after all."

"Well, curse my cannon," said Granny Leatherhead. "His name should be Admiral Reckless!"

The ISS *Colossus* was like a flying fortress, with laser cannon wide enough to park shuttles inside. But even the super-destroyer looked like a tiny speck next to the mighty black hole.

"Nichelle, take us in closer," instructed Granny Leatherhead. "Circle the outer rim. Make it as difficult as possible for them to board us."

"Aye, Captain."

Granny Leatherhead grabbed the intercom. "How's the engine, Manik?"

"It's holding together for the moment," reported the engineer's mate. "But we shouldn't push our luck."

"Just keep it working. This is going to get choppy."

Kella gripped Jake and Nanoo tightly as the *Dark Horse* slid toward the abyss. Nichelle used the reverse thrusters to control the cargo hauler, steering the ship in a wide arc until it circled the black hole.

"Fire up the big guns," instructed Granny Leatherhead.

"Aye, Captain," said both Maaka and Woorak from the gun deck.

"Callidus, take your mooncalf Capio and see what you can find in the cargo hold. There should be some explosives down there, possibly a few space mines. Use the air lock to launch anything that might damage the warship. Don't hold back, lads—throw empty rum flasks if there's nothing else."

"Aye, Captain," said Callidus.

"What about us?" asked Jake. "Is there anything we can do?"

Granny Leatherhead turned to the three teenagers. "Nanoo, stand by to fix any shields or weapons that get damaged. Kella, prepare the medical bay. Jake, get yourself down to the engine room to help Scargus and Manik."

"Aye, Captain."

The three of them left the bridge to attend to their respective stations. Jake hurried down the stairs to the lower deck. He was both terrified and excited at the same time but determined to be brave. As Jake reached the engine room, the captain's voice boomed through the corridor speakers.

"Prepare to fire!"

Jake burst through the engine-room door and was greeted with flashing lights, plumes of steam, and a frenzy of activity. Scargus and Manik worked frantically on the roaring engine, as though trying to control a wild beast, while Squawk clung to his perch, cursing and flapping his wings.

"Hello, Jake lad," said Scargus, tightening a valve.

"The captain sent me to help."

Scargus threw him a metal canister. "You can start by topping up the coolant, before the engine overheats."

Jake caught the surprisingly heavy canister and got to work. The ship was shaking under the intense pull of the black hole and Jake could hear laser cannon fire. A battle was taking place and he was missing it.

"When you're finished with that, you can check the fuel cells," said Scargus.

"Is there nothing more important I can do?" asked Jake.

An explosion outside rocked the *Dark Horse*, causing tools to escape their hooks and fly across the engine room, narrowly missing Jake's head.

"I'm sorry, Jake," said Scargus, wiping his brow with an oil-stained rag. "In a space battle, everyone has to do their bit, however big or small. We have our best pilot steering the ship and our best gunners firing the cannon. It may not be exciting down here, but the engine is essential for our survival."

Jake did as he was told but kept an eye on the battle through a grubby porthole window. The *Dark*

Horse was circling so close to the black hole, its hull skimmed the surface. Judging by the sparks and mechanical roar coming from the engine, Nichelle was using every drop of power to stop them crossing the point of no return.

As he finished checking the fuel cells, the ISS *Colossus* drew level and unleashed its laser cannon.

"Fire!" shouted Granny Leatherhead through the intercom. "Fire, you dogs, fire!"

Both ships spat out bolt after bolt, but most of them were knocked off target by the gravitational pull of the black hole. Time itself seemed to distort, as though the battle was being fought in slow motion. A few shots found their mark and pounded the other ship's shields. Nanoo had not been exaggerating about the sawed-off laser cannon, which now packed a serious punch.

Admiral Nex was so desperate to capture Jake, he was throwing everything he had at them. He dispatched six naval shuttles to board the *Dark Horse*, but each of them was sucked into the black hole the moment they launched, their weak engines unable to resist its pull. Then came troops in space suits. They were attached to lifelines and armed with laser cutters, but they quickly followed the shuttles into the black hole, leaving their cables trailing like anchors.

Jake completed job after job in the engine room to the best of his ability, but he was unable to take his eyes off the space battle outside the porthole window. Callidus and Capio had located the high explosives, which now tumbled from the air lock into the path of the ISS *Colossus*.

Boom!

The explosives detonated, catching the side of the warship and causing its hull to dip into the black hole. A section of midnight-blue metal disappeared from view, causing the super-destroyer to reduce its speed.

"Good work, boys," said Granny Leatherhead over the intercom. "That got their attention."

Despite their different sizes, both ships were suffering now. In the engine room, more and more red lights flashed on the various control panels. Jake was sure that the engine would not hold out much longer.

"Time to leave," announced Granny Leatherhead. "Nichelle, get us out of here."

"Aye, Captain."

The *Dark Horse* creaked and moaned as it attempted to break free from the gravitational pull, while the mechanical roar of the engine changed to a deafening scream.

"Scargus, we need more muscle," said Granny Leatherhead, barely audible over the noise.

"It's no good," shouted Scargus. "We're at maximum throttle."

"Blast, blast, and triple blast," she cursed. "We're stuck and our shields are getting shredded. If we don't get out of here soon, we never will."

Chapter 21

Scuppered

Jake had an idea. He grabbed the intercom off Scargus.

"Captain, we have to lighten the ship," he shouted over the noise of the engine. "The pull of the black hole is making everything heavier. When Scargus threw me a canister of coolant, it flew through the air, instead of floating. We need to make the ship lighter, so the engine doesn't have to work as hard."

"Kid Cutler, you're a genius!" said Granny Leatherhead. "Listen up, everyone. If you're not steering the ship, firing a gun, or fixing something, I want you to gather any nonessential items and take them to the cargo hold, the heavier the better."

Capio was struggling to keep up. "But I thought everything was weightless in space."

"We're not in normal space, numbskull," snapped Granny Leatherhead. "We're caught in a gravity field, so every ounce makes a difference to our thrust."

"In that case," said Callidus, "we should ditch the naval shuttle."

"Do you know how much money we could get for that shuttle?" protested Farid.

"It won't be worth anything if the *Dark Horse* is destroyed with the shuttle inside it," Callidus pointed out.

"He's right," said Granny Leatherhead. "Dump it!"

Jake and the others got to work filling the cargo hold. Spare parts, kitchen equipment, cabinets, tables, chairs, even Squawk's metal perch, were piled on top of the naval shuttle.

Jake knew that time was running out. The ship was being pushed to its limits. He could hear the engine threatening to explode and the corridor walls buckling under pressure. If they lost power now, they would be dragged into the crushing depths of the black hole.

"Stand clear," shouted Farid, throwing in a crate of rum and sealing the hatch.

"I hope this lot smashes a window in the admiral's quarters," said Capio.

The loading ramp opened and the items toppled into space, where they were instantly consumed by the black hole. Jake felt the cargo hauler jerk forward in response, freed from the excess weight.

"It's working," he said, checking a porthole window.

The *Dark Horse* crept steadily forward, forcing its way free from the black hole and leaving the naval warship behind them.

"Why aren't they following us?" asked Jake. "Are they in trouble?"

"Maybe they're too heavy to pull free," said Farid.

Callidus was doubtful. "Let's not assume anything. That's a very powerful ship."

A moment later, the ISS *Colossus* wrenched itself from the black hole and started gaining on the *Dark Horse*.

"We can't match their thrust," said Nichelle over the intercom. "They're closing on us."

"Keep going," encouraged Granny Leatherhead. "We're almost clear of the gravity field."

"It's no good." Nichelle's voice trembled with panic. "We'll never make it. They're going to ram us."

It seemed that Admiral Nex was determined to take out the *Dark Horse* by whatever means necessary. The ISS *Colossus* was moments away from crushing the damaged cargo hauler under its hull.

"We need to go faster," said Jake. "What else can we throw overboard?"

Farid shook his head. "There isn't anything, unless we ditch the laser cannon."

"No, that would leave us defenseless," said Callidus. "Is there nothing else?"

"Not really."

"Farid?"

"All right, there might be something, but I'll be skinned alive for telling you."

"We'll die if you don't," said Jake.

Farid glanced at Kodan, who nodded.

"Okay, there's a secret compartment under the stairs," confessed the first mate. "It contains three crates of heavy metals."

"What kind of metals?" asked Callidus.

"Gold bars and other valuables," said Farid. "It's all the treasure we've collected over the years, and one of the crates is Granny Leatherhead's personal retirement fund. If she finds out that I told you, she'll rip out my heart and replace it with a palm grenade."

Farid led the others to a concealed hatch, where they removed the heavy crates and dragged them to the air lock.

"If this doesn't work, nothing will," he said, sealing the inner hatch and activating the outer door.

The crates tumbled into space. Jake felt the *Dark Horse* surge forward and they all cheered.

"Hey, where did the ISS *Colossus* go?" asked Callidus, checking the porthole window.

Jake blinked at the now-empty glass.

"It was there a moment ago," said Farid.

Kodan shrugged his shoulders.

"I can still see it." Jake pointed to a dark patch outside the window. "But its lights have gone out."

"The circuits must still be damaged from the kalmar explosion," said Callidus. "And the gravity field will have drained their reserve power."

"It won't be long before the ISS *Colossus* gets sucked inside," said Jake.

They watched the warship sink into the blackness, like a sailing boat being claimed by the sea. A few lights flashed and flickered as the crew of the ISS *Colossus* attempted to restore power, but it was too late. The final sections of hull slipped from sight, lost to the gap in the stars. The ISS *Colossus* was gone forever.

Nobody spoke aboard the *Dark Horse*, partly out of respect for the dead, but also in disbelief that they had taken on the Interstellar Navy's most advanced super-destroyer and survived. Despite the odds, the small rusty mollusk had slain the giant metal shark. The crew would have reached for the rum in celebration, if they hadn't just thrown it overboard. Not a sound could be heard above the engine, no explosions or laser cannon, nothing except the sound of heavy footsteps as Granny Leatherhead stomped down the corridor toward them. "What have you mutinous morons done?" she shrieked. "That blasted black hole has swallowed my gold!"

Farid winced, as though he was certain that Granny Leatherhead was about to make them all walk the air lock.

"I'll feed the lot of you to a kalmar," she fumed, brandishing her cutlass. "It's taken me decades to amass that much treasure. Do you know how many shipmates died to get it? I said to dump *non*essential items overboard. You should have thrown yourselves into space instead. I bet that lump Kodan weighs as much as a crate of gold."

Jake couldn't really blame her for being angry— after all, her life savings had just been flushed down a cosmic toilet—but before Granny Leatherhead could say anything else, Nichelle interrupted.

"Minefield!"

Jake checked the porthole window and spotted several spiked space mines scattered around the ship.

"Take evasive action," ordered Granny Leatherhead. "Curse that coward, Nex."

The *Dark Horse* changed direction so fast, it knocked Jake off his feet and into the air. He pulled himself back to the window in time to see the nearest mine start to move toward them.

"Heat seekers," snarled Granny Leatherhead. "And one of them is locked onto our exhausts."

Nichelle was a skilled pilot, but even she would struggle to shake off a heat-seeking mine.

"Why don't we turn off the engine?" asked Jake.

"That won't work," said Callidus. "It would catch us before the exhausts cooled down."

The ship veered twice more, followed by the heat seeker. Jake watched it edge nearer and nearer.

"I can't shake it," shouted Nichelle. "It's going to hit us."

"Hold on, everyone," warned Granny Leatherhead. "Here it comes."

Boom!

The mine connected with the hull and exploded, sending the *Dark Horse* spiraling out of control. Jake was thrown across the corridor. The last thing he remembered was a sharp pain as his head bounced off the metal wall. After that, his vision blurred and the darkness consumed him.

"Hey, kiddo?" echoed a voice in Jake's head. "Can you hear me?"

Was he dreaming?

"Wake up, kiddo."

Jake felt something slip over his face and a cold sensation tickle his nostrils.

"Come on, open your eyes."

Jake did as he was told, but it took a surprising amount of effort. As far as he could tell, he was aboard the *Dark Horse*, only the temperature was ice-cold. How long had he been unconscious?

Torches and helmet lamps danced around in the darkness. Someone adjusted the oxygen mask that covered his face. He shivered and rubbed his throbbing head. There was something wet and sticky in his hair. Blood.

"Good lad, we nearly lost you for a moment."

The person helping him wore a dirty orange exploration suit and a space helmet with a grimy glass visor, through which Jake could see he was chewing gum.

"Baden Scott?" Jake recognized the salvage captain.

"Just breathe and try not to talk," said Baden. "We were returning from the shipmaker's on Reus, when our scanners registered the explosion—"

"The explosion!" Jake suddenly remembered what had happened. "Are the others okay?"

"No talking," insisted Baden. "My crew is seeing

to your friends. Your ship's systems are down and there's very little air remaining, so we're taking everyone aboard our ship for now. Are you able to walk?"

Jake nodded, and Baden helped him to his feet. He caught his reflection in the porthole window and was shocked to see a large gash parting his matted hair. In the torchlight, his skin looked white and ghoulish.

"Come on," said Baden, assisting him along the corridor to the air lock.

Jake noticed a brand-new salvage trawler outside docked with the *Dark Horse*. The name *Rough Diamond III* was printed on the side. Its glistening red hull was fitted with state-of-the-art solar panels and tinted porthole windows.

"Nice ship."

Baden opened the air-lock door and they went through to the *Rough Diamond III*. It was so clean and bright, Jake had to shield his eyes. He wasn't used to the light, or the heat, or the artificial-gravity system. His numb fingers tingled sharply as sensation returned. Baden left him resting on a padded bench and returned to the *Dark Horse*. Jake waited anxiously for the rest of the crew to transfer across.

Farid and Kodan stepped through the air-lock

door first. Callidus and Capio were close behind, followed by Maaka and Woorak. Nichelle hobbled into the light, supported by Kella, who was clutching her medical kit.

"Here, let me take a look at you," said Kella, noticing Jake's wounded head. She slapped on some antiseptic lotion, which stung like burning acid. He was about to complain when the air-lock door opened again.

"Make way." Jake recognized Kiki, the salvage crew's pilot, who was accompanied by her shipmates, Reinhart and Gunnar.

Scargus and Nanoo were carried onto the *Rough Diamond III* unconscious, their skin and clothes blackened with soot. They were rushed to the medical bay, followed by Kella. Manik limped through the air-lock door after them, holding Squawk.

"We're lucky to be alive," said Farid. "That space mine should have killed us on impact."

"It was Nanoo," said Manik. "That boy is a hero."

"How come?" asked Jake.

"He activated his personal force field at the last second. It shielded us from the explosion and contained the damage. If it hadn't been for Nanoo, we'd all be dead now. His quick thinking saved the ship."

Granny Leatherhead was the last to leave the *Dark Horse*. Baden helped her through the air-lock door.

"Thank you, Captain," she croaked, holding a bloodied rag under her hooked nose. "If you hadn't come along when you did, we would be kalmar bait by now."

"No problem," he said. "Let's call it even, seeing as I owed you a favor anyway."

"Me?" Granny Leatherhead eyed him curiously. "I don't recall us ever meeting."

"Well, not you personally." Baden corrected himself. "It was the Novu boy who did me a good turn. He let me have the remains of his ship, which contained some rare alien technology. I made enough money to buy this vessel and a holiday home on Reus."

"Is that so?" Granny Leatherhead shot Callidus a dirty look. "I had no idea the wreck was worth so much. Nanoo was very generous to give it away."

Callidus ignored her and wrapped an emergency blanket around his shoulders. Jake knew that a new salvage trawler and a holiday home on Reus were nothing when compared with a gold-covered planet and three crystal moons. For Callidus, it had always been about Altus.

* * *

A few hours later, everyone was feeling much better aboard the *Rough Diamond III*, including Scargus and Nanoo, who had opened their eyes. Gunnar helped to fix the engine on the *Dark Horse*, but it was only a temporary patch job to get the cargo hauler to the next service port. Baden insisted on giving them a small backup generator in case of emergencies.

Jake wanted to go before the salvage captain realized they were space pirates. He was surprised that Baden hadn't already noticed the open gun ports and pirate markings. Jake was also worried that the Space Dogs might try to spacejack the *Rough Diamond III* if they stayed much longer.

It turned out that Granny Leatherhead was just as keen as Jake to leave, before any more warships showed up. The Interstellar Navy would know that the ISS *Colossus* had been pursuing the *Dark Horse* when it disappeared.

"Thank you once again, Captain," she croaked, shaking Baden's hand. "You saved my ship and my crew, but now we must be on our way, because we have cargo to deliver."

"Wait, I still don't know what happened," he said. "Why were you attacked? What happened to the other ship? Does this have something to do with Altus?"

"No, it's nothing that exciting," she lied. "A bunch of spacejackers thought we were carrying crystals and attacked us. Their ship flew too close to the black hole and got sucked inside, but not before they took out our engine."

"It sounds as though you were lucky," said Baden, scratching his stubble. "Perhaps it would be best if we escorted you to the next service port."

"Thank you, that's a kind offer, but you've already done so much for us."

Jake and the crew stepped into the air lock, followed by Granny Leatherhead. "Cheers, Captain, until we meet again."

"Good-bye, Captain," said Baden, stuffing more gum into his mouth. "Don't worry, when I report the black hole, I won't tell the Interstellar Navy which way you went. You see, my salvage operation may be legitimate, but my ancestors were from Zerost."

Granny Leatherhead gave him a knowing smile and disappeared into her ship. By the time they reached the bridge, the two vessels had already drifted apart.

"Let's see if this old rust bucket works," she said, rubbing her hands. "Nichelle, resume our original course."

"Aye, Captain."

Nichelle tested the engine with a few bursts of thrust before accelerating away from the *Rough Diamond III*. The cargo hauler creaked a little more than usual, but the ship held together as it gathered speed. No one was sorry to leave the black hole behind.

Chapter 22

The Tego Nebula

The *Dark Horse* cruised through space, avoiding the main trade routes. They were heading for Papa Don's to continue their search for Altus. Scargus and Manik fussed over the engine like anxious parents, while Nanoo repaired the ship's defenses. Most of the crew relaxed in their quarters, but not Jake. He wandered aimlessly about the ship with his handheld computer tucked under his arm, lost in thought.

Jake felt responsible for putting the others in danger. If it wasn't for him and his gold pendant, they wouldn't be on the run from the Interstellar Navy. Too many people had died already. How many more would be forced to suffer?

Jake was so distracted, he didn't realize where he was going until he walked on to the bridge.

Granny Leatherhead was sulking in the captain's chair. She hadn't gotten over the fact that they had thrown away her gold. Farid and the others had assured her that there hadn't been any other way to escape the black hole, but she refused to listen, claiming there was no point growing a day older without her retirement fund.

"It'll be okay," said Jake.

"Will it?" Granny Leatherhead said, and glared at him. "What do you know about it, you pint-sized pain-in-the-aft? You've been nothing but trouble since you set foot on my ship."

"When we find Altus, I'll pay you double the amount you've lost."

"Double, eh?" She scratched her eye patch with a clawlike finger. "I like the sound of that, your short-ness, but what if we can't locate your precious planet? What will you do for me then?"

"I'll stay on this ship until I've paid you back," said Jake. "But it won't come to that. We'll find my planet, I know it."

Granny Leatherhead seemed to deflate, as though the fight had been knocked out of her. For the first time, the tough pirate captain looked like a fragile old woman.

"I can't spend your faith," she said, and withdrew to her quarters.

Jake stared at the crystals on his gold pendant, hoping the answer would leap out at him, but they just sat there sparkling in the dim light. What was it that he was supposed to know? What made him so special? How could he unlock the secret location of his home planet, when so many others had failed?

Whatever the answer, Jake had to figure it out quickly. The crew had just destroyed the Interstellar Navy's best warship, making them the most wanted pirates in the seven solar systems. The Space Dogs needed a place to hide and fast.

"Hey, Nichelle. Is it much farther to Papa Don's?"

"Not far now." The pilot sat hunched over the controls with her eyes fixed on the main display. "We got lucky and caught a space wave."

"A what?"

"A space wave," she said. "When a sun flares up, it creates an invisible force that ripples through space, a sort of solar tide. We've been riding a space wave for the last hour."

"Oh, right." Jake attempted to flop into the empty seat, but instead fell in slow motion, like a leaf from a tree. He sighed.

"Is everything okay?"

"Yeah, I suppose so," he said, holding on to the armrests.

"Really?"

"Yes, no, oh, I don't know." Jake strapped himself into the seat. "You're all expecting so much from me and I don't want to let anyone down, but what do I know about ruling a planet? I can't even remember what Altus looks like, let alone lead its people. What would you do?"

"You're asking me?" Nichelle puffed out her cheeks and blew into the air. "Listen, I'm only a pilot and I don't know any more than you about being a ruler, but I suppose I would be excited to see my long-lost relatives."

"What if they don't want to see me?"

"Garbish," she said, turning her eyes away from the screen. "Just because your uncle sounds like a total jerk, it doesn't mean the rest of your family will be the same."

Nichelle had a point. Amicus had only mentioned Kear, but there could be other Cutlers living on Altus.

"What's that?" asked Jake as something popped onto the long-range scanner. "Is that a ship?"

Nichelle took a look and smiled.

"That, my friend," she said, "is Papa Don's illegal spaceport."

The *Dark Horse* had reached the safety of the colorful Tego Nebula. Papa Don's illegal spaceport was still open for business and rotating like a giant carousel. The crew had gathered on the bridge, but Granny

Leatherhead remained in her quarters, leaving Farid in charge of the ship. Nichelle held the cargo hauler at a safe distance from the port, in case the space mafia enquired about Kella.

"Now what?" she asked, sitting back from the controls. "Where do we start our search?"

Farid glanced at Callidus, who turned to Jake, who was skulking at the back of the bridge with his hands in his pockets. It was the moment Jake had been dreading, the moment he was supposed to come up with all the answers. He could feel the weight of expectation in the room.

"I've been thinking about nothing else," he said, as everyone gathered around him. "I know that Altus exists, but I just don't know how to find it."

There was an awkward silence, which seemed to last forever, before Capio spoke.

"All this time studying that cursed pendant and you still don't have a clue? Not even the slightest inclination?"

Jake shrugged. "I'm sorry."

"You're sorry?" Capio twitched slightly. "I've had to put up with space pirates, naval warships, illegal spaceports, alien shipwrecks, and tentacled monsters . . . all for nothing?"

"Jake, are you sure there isn't something you've

missed?" asked Callidus. "A minor detail in your past that you might have overlooked?"

Jake tried to think, but it was difficult to concentrate under so much pressure.

"Well?" pressed Farid.

"Yeah, come on," said Capio. "Let's hear it."

The crew closed in around Jake, casting him in shadow.

"It's not his fault," said Kella, standing next to him. "He never claimed to know the location."

"Yes, give Jake chance," urged Nanoo, joining them. "He work it out."

"Hey, that's not a bad idea. We can work it out," said Kella, pointing to the handheld computer. "Jake, you lived with cyber-monks. Don't they use technology to solve problems?"

"I've already tried," he sighed. "But there's nothing logical about Altus."

"Well, let's try again," she said, snatching the handheld computer and tapping the screen. "Tell me what to do."

Jake knew it was pointless to argue with her.

"Okay," he said. "First, we need to establish the facts. Fact one, we don't know the location of Altus."

Kella gave him a reproachful look and then typed as she talked. "Fact two, the Interstellar Navy believes that Altus is somewhere between Remota and Papa Don's spaceport."

"Fact three," said Callidus. "Jake's gold pendant and the Altian shipwreck contained the same symbol: three circles inside a larger circle with a swirling border."

Kella paused for further input.

"Anyone else?"

None of the crew spoke.

"Fact four, we believe in you, Jake Cutler," croaked a voice in the doorway.

Jake turned to see Granny Leatherhead standing by the hatch, dressed in her full pirate outfit and holding her skull-shaped space helmet.

"You do?"

"Yes," she said, blinking at him. "I'm counting on you to put these clues together and replace my retirement fund. Don't let me down, Kid Cutler."

The crowd parted to give Jake room to think. He wandered over to the main display and stared hard at Papa Don's. Was there something special about the space mafia and their illegal spaceport? What secrets were held within those curved metal walls? It looked so peaceful and unassuming suspended in front of the Tego Nebula, framed by its golden corona, like a crown of light.

"That's it," he cried, his purple eyes bursting with excitement. "I know where to find Altus."

"Just like that?" said Capio.

"But we haven't finished making the calculations," protested Kella, waving the handheld computer.

Granny Leatherhead joined Jake at the main display. "Does it have something to do with Papa Don's?"

"No, it's behind the spaceport," said Jake.

"But there's nothing there except—"

"Yes, that's right." Jake grinned. "Altus is inside the Tego Nebula."

"What?" said Farid. "Inside it?"

Jake pointed to the image of the Tego Nebula on the main display. "Do you see its corona? Amicus Kent said that not every cloud has a silver lining. I didn't realize what he meant until now. He's right. This cloud has a golden lining."

"So it does," said Kella. "It's beautiful."

"I had assumed the swirling border on my gold pendant was just for decoration." Jake held it up for everyone to see. "But the swirls could easily represent a cloud wrapped around a planet and its three moons."

"Yes, of course," said Callidus. "The word *Tego* means 'to conceal.' I can't believe it's been here all this time, hidden inside that cloud of space dust."

"You mean we've found it?" Capio asked. "We've located planet Altus?"

The bridge erupted with cheers and excited chatter.

"Hold on, you bunch of bandits," croaked Granny Leatherhead. "Let's not get carried away. It's a good theory, but where's the proof? How can we be certain that he's guessed it right?"

"I don't have any proof," said Jake. "Why don't we just fly into the Tego Nebula to see if Altus is inside?"

"Fly into the Tego Nebula?" exclaimed Nichelle. "I'm afraid it's not that simple, Jake. The nebula is far too dense and ionized with electricity. We would have to do everything manually."

Farid nodded in agreement. "Who knows what would happen once we were inside. If the ship got into trouble, we would be stranded."

"What other option do we have?" asked Callidus. "How long before Papa Don notices us? How long before the Interstellar Navy turns up? You were all prepared to risk everything over the black hole—is this any different?"

"Yes," said Farid. "We're being asked to risk our lives on the instincts of a thirteen-year-old boy."

Granny Leatherhead turned to Jake.

"Well, Kid Cutler?" she said. "How sure are you that there's something inside that cosmic candy floss?"

Jake glanced at the swirling clouds of the Tego Nebula, wishing he could see through them and catch a glimpse of a planet. The mass of bright colors felt familiar and calming to him.

"I'm positive," he said.

Granny Leatherhead considered this for a moment and then turned to Nichelle.

"Set a course for the heart of the nebula."

"But . . . aye, Captain."

The *Dark Horse* moved past the illegal spaceport to the edge of the Tego Nebula, which was far greater than anything else they had encountered. Nichelle made disapproving noises each time the lights flickered, and she swore out loud when the scanners scrambled.

"This is impossible," she protested. "It's suicide. There could be anything inside that cloud and we wouldn't know until we hit it."

"Nichelle's right," said Farid. "The ship is still damaged from our battle with the ISS *Colossus*. It would only take one stray asteroid to wreck us."

Callidus nodded thoughtfully. "Technology can't help us on this occasion, but there might be another way."

He turned to Capio and smiled.

"Whatever you're thinking, the answer is no," said his curly-haired companion. "I mean it, Cal. I've had enough of your reckless stunts. No, no, no, absolutely not."

Chapter 23

The Lost Planet

Callidus and Capio stood in the air lock dressed in space suits, while Jake helped Maaka Metal Head to check their helmets.

"Here we go again, throwing ourselves into space," complained Capio.

"Trust me, this will work," said Callidus. "I've kept us alive this long, haven't I?"

"Yes, but it's you who keeps putting us in danger. Tell me it's still about the crystals, Cal. We must have earned our reward by now."

Jake and Maaka stepped outside and sealed the inner hatch. Two amber lights flashed on the ceiling and the outer air-lock door cracked open.

Capio swept up his lifeline. "I really hate the universe sometimes."

"You'd better get moving," said Granny Leatherhead over the intercom. "Farid has picked up a couple of naval warships on the long-range scanners."

Jake watched the two men leave the air lock and then he headed back to the bridge. By the time he reached the top deck, Callidus and Capio had already climbed onto the nose of the ship, where they sat holding the tow cable. The static from the nebula blocked their helmet communicators, forcing them to use a more basic form of contact. Callidus flashed his helmet lamp and waited for Farid to return the signal with a torch.

The plan was as simple as it was daring. Callidus and Capio would guide the cargo hauler through the Tego Nebula, staying in front of the ship and feeling their way through the thick clouds. They would remain connected to the tow cable to avoid getting lost. If they came across anything unusual, they would use their helmet lamps to warn the others: one flash to slow down, two to stop, three to proceed, and four for danger. It would be slow progress, but better to be cautious than dead.

With a final wave, Callidus and Capio launched themselves off the hull and propelled themselves with bursts of compressed air from two spare oxygen tanks. The two men disappeared into the nebula, leaving only the slack tow cable visible. Nichelle gave her throttle a gentle nudge and the *Dark Horse* drifted after them, its nose parting the multicolored fog.

"Keep watch for their helmet lamps," said Farid as angry bolts of electricity streamed by the windows. "We're reliant on Callidus and Capio to find the safest route. A move in the wrong direction could be fatal."

"Let's hope there aren't any kalmars in this space smog," croaked Granny Leatherhead. "Those two would make a tasty snack."

"I not think anything survive long in nebula without space suit," said Nanoo, watching the clouds through his X-ray device. "Not even space monsters."

For several minutes the *Dark Horse* edged forward without hindrance. Nichelle did her best to maintain a straight course, but there was no way to be sure. Jake kept watch for signs of Callidus and Capio, catching the occasional hint of an arm or leg at the end of the tow cable. He tried not to blink for fear of missing a signal.

"I see something," said Nanoo. "A light."

"Yes, I saw it too," confirmed Kella.

"How many?" asked Farid.

"There was a single flash," said Jake.

Kella and Nanoo nodded in agreement.

"Okay, slow down, Nichelle," instructed Granny Leatherhead. "Let's take it steady until we know what's out there."

"Aye, Captain."

It was impossible to tell how fast they were traveling through the clouds. According to their faulty instruments, they were either not moving at all or they had broken the light barrier, neither of which was likely.

"What's that?" asked Jake, spotting a dark shadow ahead.

The gloomy shape swelled before their eyes, as though growing out of the nebula.

"Two flashes!" cried Kella. "I saw two flashes of light."

"Stop the ship," ordered Granny Leatherhead.

"Aye, Captain."

Nichelle slammed on the reverse thrusters just in time to avoid a major collision. The *Dark Horse* nudged gently into the mysterious object with a deep metallic thud. In front of the cargo hauler, Callidus and Capio were clinging to a large chromium cylinder suspended in the clouds. It was too small to be a spaceship and too large to be an escape pod.

"I hope it's not some kind of s-s-space mine," stuttered Woorak.

"It's just a probe," said Granny Leatherhead. "Most likely launched from a science vessel to take samples from the nebula. It must have been struck by lightning before it could return."

"It's eerie." Kella shuddered. "It looks so sad and lonely stuck in this cloud."

"I wonder how long it's been here," said Jake.

"Difficult to say." Farid moved closer to the window. "It could be old, really old, not to mention valuable. We should take it with us, in case we can't find it again."

"No, we shouldn't," said Granny Leatherhead. "The more time we waste in this death dust, the more likely we'll be hit by lightning. Let's leave the probe, before we get trapped here with it."

Farid flashed his torch three times, signaling to Callidus and Capio to move forward again. The two men launched themselves back into the cloud and melted out of sight. Nichelle squeezed the thrusters and steered around the probe, following Callidus and Capio into the unknown.

"Hey, what that?" asked Nanoo, pointing at Jake's chest.

Jake looked down to find his top glowing.

"Your pendant," gasped Kella.

Jake pulled it out. The gold object sparkled with light, its bright colors reflecting off windows and display screens. It was as though the three crystals had come alive, filling the room with their brilliance.

"Incredible," said Farid. "How did you get it to do that?"

"I didn't." Jake was just as surprised as everyone else. "I didn't do anything."

"Don't look at me," said Kella. "I've not touched it."

"Maybe crystals react to cloud electricity," suggested Nanoo. "Static make my skin feel funny."

Jake held the pendant in his hand. *What a curious object*, he thought. All those years it had hung around his neck and never before had it lit up. What other secrets did it hold? He ran his fingers over the glowing crystals and something in the pendant clicked. He turned it over and discovered a crack running right round the edge. It seemed to be splitting in two. Was that supposed to happen?

Carefully, Jake pried the pendant open with his nails.

It was a locket and there was something hidden inside. He stared at the contents in disbelief.

"What inside?" asked Nanoo, trying to catch a glimpse. "Secret technology?"

"Or a rare jewel?" croaked Granny Leatherhead.

"How about a treasure map?" asked Farid.

"No, it's none of those things," said Jake, holding up his pendant for all to see. "It's an old photograph."

Inside the locket was a picture of a young woman with chalk-white skin, ivory blonde hair, and blood-red eyes. The woman sat in front of a window, bathed in bright-colored light.

"She's beautiful," said Kella. "Who is she?"

"I think she's my mom." Jake took another look at the image. "I have no memory of her, but there's something familiar about her face."

"There's definitely a family resemblance," said Granny Leatherhead. "If you ask me, you have the same smile."

"I've never seen such stunning red eyes," remarked Farid.

Jake didn't hear them. He was too captivated by the tiny photo. He had always wondered what his parents looked like, and here was a picture of his mother, Zara Cutler, happy and full of life. He ran his finger over her pretty face and tried to imagine the sound of her voice.

"It would make sense for you to have a picture of your mother," said Granny Leatherhead. "But that doesn't explain why your pendant has suddenly activated."

"Maybe Nanoo is right and the crystals are react-ing to the ionized atmosphere," said Farid.

"It's not just his pendant." Nichelle pointed

to the window. "The whole nebula is getting brighter."

Around the ship, the clouds had become lighter and more transparent. Jake could now make out the shapes of Callidus and Capio floundering in the mist. It took him a moment to realize they were waving their arms and flashing their helmet lamps.

"Two flashes," he cried. "Stop the ship."

"He's right," shouted Granny Leatherhead. "Avast, Nichelle, pull back."

It was too late. The whole ship started to rock.

"What's happening?" asked Kella, losing her balance. "It feels like we're falling."

"That's because we are," said Farid. "Quick, everyone, grab hold of something! We're entering a gravity field."

"More black hole?" asked Nanoo.

"No, this is different," said Nichelle. "It's the sort of gravity generated by a planet."

"Altus," whispered Jake.

The *Dark Horse* burst out of the nebula clouds into colorful skies, no longer supported by zero gravity.

"It so bright," said Nanoo, shielding his eyes.

Jake squinted at the screen. "We're heading straight for the surface!"

"I know," said Nichelle, slipping on sunglasses and wrestling with the controls.

The *Dark Horse* didn't perform well as an aircraft. It was only designed for simple landings and launches. Jake could hear the engine moaning and the hull rattling as Nichelle pulled the ship into a rough orbit. His eyes adjusted to the light and feasted on the planet below them. It could only be Altus.

His Altus.

Home.

It was as beautiful as the legends described, a secret paradise hidden in the stars. He marveled at the perfect sphere, which sparkled with a gold-dust desert and blue ocean water. Three crystal moons surrounded the planet: one diamond, one ruby, and one emerald. Powered by the nebula, the moons radiated light and warmth to the surface below.

"Magnifty," said Jake, unable to blink for fear of missing something.

Kella and Nanoo nodded in agreement, their eyes wide and their mouths agape.

"Scuttle my shuttle," said Farid. "It's just like Callidus imagined—"

"Callidus!"

Jake had forgotten about the fortune seeker and his companion. He pressed his face up against the window, but the two men were no longer in front of the ship.

"Where did they go?" asked Kella.

Granny Leatherhead activated the intercom. "Maaka, check the tow cable. Are our friends still attached to the other end?"

There was a brief silence before Maaka reported back.

"Aye, Captain," he said. "Neither of them look very happy, but they're still with us, hanging on for their lives."

"Well, don't just stand there, you metal-faced marauder!" she bellowed. "Reel them back in."

A short while later, Callidus and Capio were back on the bridge of the *Dark Horse*. They were a bit battered and bruised, but otherwise fine. When Capio caught sight of the three crystal moons through the window, he forgot about the pain and almost exploded with delight.

"Look at those giant jewels," he squealed. "It's real, Cal. Altus is real and we found it."

"Yes, we did," said Callidus, his blue eyes soaking up the view. "And it's exactly how I imagined it."

"So what happens now?" asked Jake.

"Isn't it obvious?" said Callidus. "We prepare to land."

*　　*　　*

"Today we have made space pirate history," announced Granny Leatherhead to everyone on the bridge. "This crew has succeeded where others have failed. We've found the legendary Altus."

A few shipmates whistled and stamped their feet.

"Now comes the tough part," she said. "We've got a planet to spacejack, so young Jake can take his rightful place as ruler. This means finding Kear Cutler and removing him from power, only we don't know what's waiting for us below. I want you to keep your wits about you. Let's get to work, Space Dogs."

"Aye!" cheered the crew.

Granny Leatherhead turned to Farid. "What have you found out?"

"There are no obvious defenses," said the first mate. "I've not seen any Altian ships and we haven't passed any observation stations or atmospheric mines. If there is a planetary guard, it's not expecting an invasion any time soon."

It was difficult to know where best to land. If Amicus Kent was right, Kear Cutler would dispatch his troops to arrest Jake the moment he realized his nephew was alive and on Altus. Were the Space Dogs ready to take on the entire Altian army?

"We should head to the largest city," proposed Callidus. "That's where we'll find Kear Cutler."

"It would be safer to land somewhere more secluded," said Farid. "Until we know what we're facing."

"I prefer the direct approach," insisted Callidus. "We'll only have the element of surprise once, so let's not waste it."

"Why land at all?" said Capio. "Instead of risking our lives on the surface, why don't we just fill the cargo hold with moon crystals and leave? We could let the Interstellar Navy have the location of Altus in exchange for our freedom."

"Hey," shouted Jake. "That's my planet you're talking about. What about the Altian people?"

"It's not like you know any of them," said Capio. "And you certainly don't owe your uncle any favors."

"Capio, when will you learn?" said Callidus wearily. "The Interstellar Navy would never honor a deal with space pirates."

"But—"

"Silence!" barked Granny Leatherhead, holding up her hands. "You're all giving me a headache. Farid, what's outside the largest city?"

"It looks like farmland, Captain."

"That'll do nicely," she said. "Nichelle, set us down in a field, preferably near a river or stream."

"Aye, Captain."

"As for the rest of you." Granny Leatherhead cast her eye around the bridge. "You'd best get strapped in, ready for landing. It's going to be bumpy."

Chapter 24

Kear Cutler's
Reign of Terror

The *Dark Horse* plunged toward the planet's surface, its plump hull barging through the turbulent sky. Nichelle lifted the nose at the last second and fired the landing thrusters, but the ship refused to slow. It hit the ground with such force, the windows cracked and the floors buckled. The old cargo hauler bounced and scraped across the Altian farmland, gouging a trench in the mud behind it. Jake felt his bed straps digging into his flesh as the ship finally ground to a halt.

It took everyone a moment to recover.

"That could have been worse," said Callidus. "Not many pilots can land in a field."

Granny Leatherhead's voice crackled over the intercom.

"Right, I want everyone in the cargo hold in five minutes, dressed for combat and ready to go."

Callidus and Capio released their straps and climbed out of their bunks, rubbing their bruised bodies. Jake quickly took another peek at the photo inside his gold locket. Was the beautiful albino woman really his mother? What had she been like? What had she been thinking when the photo was taken? At least they had something in common. Her red eyes might have been more natural than Jake's purple implants, but she would still have known how it felt to be different.

As Jake looked at the photo, something inside the lid caught his attention. He rotated the locket toward the light and discovered a tiny engraving. It was a skull in a space helmet over two crossed bones.

"What's that doing there?" he muttered to himself.

Before he could examine it further, Callidus shook his arm.

"What are you waiting for?" asked the fortune seeker. "An invitation? Don't you want to see your home planet?"

"Yes, of course," said Jake, putting the locket away and climbing off the bed.

As he got ready, he glanced through the porthole window and saw that they had landed in a field full of crops. There were several farm buildings nearby, none of which looked particularly alien to him, except for a scattering of hexagonal panels on the rooftops that

Jake guessed must be used to harness the power of the crystal moons. In many ways, the farm was similar to those on Remota, only without the gray dust.

It had taken eleven years, but he was finally home.

In the cargo hold, the others were already lined up. It reminded Jake of the monastery attack, except this time he knew who was beneath the skull-shaped space helmets. These pirates were here to liberate Altus, not destroy it.

"Okay, the plan is simple," croaked the captain. "We find a way into the city and track down Kear Cutler, so Jake can avenge his father and take control of the planet. Farid, check everyone's weapons and hand out extra palm grenades. We leave in two minutes."

There weren't any combat suits small enough for Jake, Kella, and Nanoo, so instead they had painted the space pirate logo on their tops, which Granny Leatherhead thought was hilarious.

"Right, Space Pups," she cackled. "I hope your bite is worse than your bark."

"It's not funny," said Jake. "We don't even have weapons to defend ourselves."

"Have you ever fired a gun?"

"No, but I've been practicing with a cutlass."

"Well, you had better go and find yourself one," she said. "Just be careful where you stick it."

Scargus and Manik had agreed to remain behind to guard the ship and work on the engine.

"Here you go, Jake, take mine." Scargus handed over his cutlass. "You need this more than me."

"Thanks," said Jake. "I'll take good care of it."

"Kella, Nanoo, take these." Manik passed each of them a sword. "You'll have a fighting chance if you're attacked."

Kella and Nanoo took the weapons and swished them about to test their weight.

"Listen, you don't have to come," said Jake. "This isn't your fight."

"It's okay. We want to help," insisted Kella, stroking the side of her blade. "Don't we, Nanoo?"

"Yes, we in this together." Nanoo puffed out his chest. "You help us, so we return favor."

Jake looked at their determined faces and nodded. He was worried for his friends, but also pleased that they would be there to cover his back.

Granny Leatherhead watched Kella hacking the air with her sword. "Mind you don't cut yourself, prissy pants. It's not safe outside for posh United Worlds girls, you know."

"It's not safe for any of us," said Kella indignantly.

"I'm tougher than I look, Captain, and I want to do my bit."

"Why?"

"Because if it wasn't for Jake, I would be a slave by now. I'm sick of bullies pushing around my friends and family. If it's not the Galactic Trade Corporation, it's the Interstellar Navy, or the space mafia. I've had enough of space thugs and I want to fight back."

Granny Leatherhead regarded Kella with something that resembled pride.

"You've got gumption, girl," she croaked. "You remind me of my daughter, Jenny. She would have made a good pirate captain, had things worked out differently."

"Your daughter?" said Kella. "What happened to her?"

"Not every buccaneer makes it to retirement," muttered Granny Leatherhead sadly.

With that, the captain turned sharply and activated the loading ramp. It cracked open with a slow mechanical whine, flooding the cargo hold with colored light and fresh air. Jake took a deep breath and held it. He had become used to the stale odor of the ship and was surprised how sweet the Altian air tasted.

"Let's go, Space Dogs," barked Granny Leatherhead.

The crew stomped down the metal ramp, weapons at the ready. Jake, Kella, and Nanoo followed behind.

A crowd of people had gathered around the cargo hauler. Jake assumed they were Altians, but they could have been from any planet in the seven solar systems. They seemed very interested in Nanoo and were pointing at him, making comments about his lilac skin.

"Greetings," said one of the farmers, stepping forward. "My name is John Daxton. Are you from outside the nebula?"

"What of it?" Granny Leatherhead gripped her laser pistol.

"Forgive us for staring, but we've never seen outsiders." John wore a tall straw hat and spoke with the same clipped accent as Amicus Kent. "We've heard stories of other worlds, but it's been such a long time since anyone left the nebula."

"Are you undertakers?" asked a woman holding a rake.

"What?" said Granny Leatherhead.

"Well, you've got skull-shaped hats and a skeleton on your spacecraft." The woman had clearly never seen space pirates. "Is that your funeral vessel?"

"No, it's not," said Granny Leatherhead. "And

we're not undertakers . . . but death does feature in our line of work."

Callidus quickly changed the subject. "Tell me, is this Altus?"

"Yes, that's right," said John. "Have you lost your way?"

"A little. We're looking for Kear Cutler."

A few of the Altians exchanged nervous glances and shuffled their feet.

"Are you friends?" asked John.

"Not exactly," said Callidus. "We're here on business."

"Is he dead?"

"Not yet," muttered Granny Leatherhead.

"Did they say Kear Cutler is dead?" asked an elderly farmhand, mishearing the exchange, and sparking frantic gossip.

"Are you here to collect his body?" the woman wondered.

"We're *not* undertakers," said Callidus, trying to restore calm. "And your ruler is alive and well, as far as we know."

"It takes more than a title to rule," snorted the woman, who was quickly silenced by John.

"Forgive us," he said. "We're just simple country folk and we know little about politics. Hilary, my wife, meant nothing by that comment. We live to serve."

"Really?" scoffed Farid. "If you ask me, Kear Cutler doesn't seem very popular in these parts."

"No, not at all. We love our leader." John dropped to his knees and encouraged others to do the same. "Long live Kear Cutler, ruler of Altus."

Granny Leatherhead had heard enough. "Get up, you yellow-bellied yokels. We don't care what you think about that jumped-up jackass, we just want to know where to find him."

The Altians stopped cowering and stared at Granny Leatherhead, their mouths wide open. Apparently, nobody had ever called Kear Cutler a jackass, especially not one who was "jumped-up," whatever that meant.

"Please, don't be afraid," said Jake, stepping forward and helping the farmer to his feet. "Nobody is going to hurt you."

John regarded him curiously, but Jake was used to people staring at his bright-purple eyes. The farmer lowered his gaze and gasped.

"It can't be . . ."

"I'm sorry?" said Jake. "Oh, the skull and crossbones? Don't worry, it's just a picture."

"Where did you get that?" John pointed at Jake's chest.

The crystals were still shining through Jake's top. He pulled out the pendant and held it up, attracting further gasps from the crowd.

"I've had it for as long as I can remember," he said.

"Is it possible?" John dropped back onto his knees. "Can it really be the lost seal of Altus after all this time?"

"The what?" asked Granny Leatherhead.

"The seal of Altus," said John. "The rulers of Altus have always possessed three unique items, including this seal. It's the key to the planet, the symbol of power."

"Three items?" asked Granny Leatherhead. "What were the other two?"

"A crown and a sword, both made of gold and encrusted with jewels," said John. "For centuries they have been passed down to each successor, until Andras Cutler left the nebula with them and never returned. Kear is the first person to rule without them."

Andras Cutler had never returned. Jake's shoulders sank. He had so desperately hoped to find his father waiting for him on Altus.

"Do you know what happened to Andras?" asked Callidus.

"Kear claimed his brother was killed in a space accident, along with his crew and only child," said

Hilary, her voice a whisper, "but how could he know that?"

John nodded in agreement. "When their ship failed to return, Kear seized power and forbade anyone else to leave Altus. He told us that he'd found evidence of a conspiracy, that Andras was planning to betray us and we were well rid of him."

"That's garbish," shouted Jake angrily. "My dad wasn't a traitor. Kear Cutler is a liar. He sabotaged our ship."

"Your dad?" said the farmer. "Your ship?"

There was little point in trying to deny it.

"Yes, that's right. I'm Jake Cutler, son of Andras. I've come to take my place as the rightful ruler of Altus and make my uncle pay for what he has done."

A stunned silence was followed by nervous muttering. Jake watched the anxious farmers and wondered if he had done the right thing. It was obvious that Kear had some sort of hold over these people. Were they frightened enough to alert the Altian army?

"Nice one, mighty mouth," hissed Granny Leatherhead. "There goes our element of surprise. Now there's only one way you'll get to meet Kear."

"Which is?" asked Jake.

"Dead."

* * *

The next morning, two hover-trucks joined the usual procession of traffic along the main route to Karmadon, the capital of Altus. At first glance they appeared to be old farm vehicles heading to market, but there was something unusual about them. Both trucks were painted black and decorated with large white skulls. This instantly attracted the attention of the city guards.

"Halt," commanded the most senior guard, stepping out in front of the hover-trucks. "What business do you have in Karmadon?"

Granny Leatherhead removed her skull-shaped space helmet and leaned out of the driver's window.

"We've come from outside the Tego Nebula," she said.

"What did you say?" The guard was visibly alarmed. "No one ever comes through that cloud. Not even our own ships these days. What brings you here?"

"We're interstellar undertakers," she lied.

"Undertakers?"

"Yes, that's right," she said. "We've brought three coffins for your ruler, Kear Cutler."

"Coffins?"

"Yes . . . Do you have to repeat everything I say?"

"I don't know how you found our planet," said the guard, straightening his maroon uniform. "But you're in luck. Any outsiders must be taken to see our glorious ruler, Kear Cutler. What makes you think he needs three coffins?"

"It's not the coffins that will interest him," she cackled. "It's what's inside them that matters. We have the bodies of Amicus Kent, Andras Cutler, and Jake Cutler, as well as the seal of Altus."

Granny Leatherhead held up a picture of Jake's pendant. The guard took one look and marched down the side of the truck, banging it with his fist.

"Open up," he demanded.

The back doors creaked opened and several Space Dogs climbed out.

"Who are you?"

"We're the pallbearers," said Farid. "We carry the coffins."

The guard peered inside the truck. "Why are there so many of you?"

"Those bodies are heavy."

"What bodies?" asked the guard. "I don't see any bodies."

"That's because they're in the other truck," said the first mate. "Don't you know it's unlucky to travel with the dead?"

Farid accompanied the guard to the second hover-truck and opened its back doors. Inside lay three wooden coffins, which looked as though they had been built in a hurry.

"I want to see the bodies," said the guard.

"Sorry, pal, no chance." Farid shut the doors. "It would take us forever to get those lids closed again. Besides, Kear Cutler should be the first to identify his brother's remains. I doubt he would take kindly to a city guard gawking at the corpse of an Altian ruler."

"I certainly wouldn't want to do anything to upset our great and noble leader," said the guard.

"Well?" shouted Granny Leatherhead from the first truck. "What's the verdict, chief?"

The guard signaled to his fellow city guards.

"We'll escort you to the Great Hall," he said. "That's the large gold building at the top of the hill."

The guard mounted a maroon hover-bike and set off, closely followed by the black trucks and two more city guards on hover-bikes. The five vehicles rejoined the flow of traffic as it poured through the city walls into the capital.

"Did you hear that, Cal?" said Capio in the back of the first truck. "A whole building made of gold. I love this planet."

Chapter 25

The Great Hall

Inside the city walls, the main road branched off into several smaller streets, and the senior guard took the route that led up the hill. Karmadon was by far the largest and most beautiful city on Altus. They passed street after street crammed with ancient architecture and exotic gardens as they headed to a magnificent building at the top. The Great Hall of Karmadon towered over the rest of the city, its gold walls and crystal spires glittering in the colored moonlight.

All five vehicles pulled up outside a set of ornately decorated gates and waited. More troops in maroon uniforms emerged from a small hut and surrounded the two hover-trucks. They wore thick body armor and carried gold-plated rifles.

"Are these the undertakers?" asked one of the troopers, who had a trimmed beard and a long cloak.

"Yes, that's right," said the city guard, saluting, before commenting to Granny Leatherhead, "Kear

Cutler's personal guards will have the honor of taking you to meet our magnificent ruler."

The bearded trooper signaled for the gates to be opened and then turned to Granny Leatherhead.

"You will come with us."

The hover-trucks were escorted across a stone courtyard to the Great Hall. The "pallbearers" were searched for weapons, before being allowed to unload the coffins and carry them into the building. They were led through a crystal-studded reception room into an enormous gold hall with stained-glass windows. Maroon flags hung from the ceiling over rows of wooden banquet tables. At the end of the hall, three giant crystals were arranged on the wall in the symbol of Altus.

"Get a load of those beauties, Cal," said Capio, whistling under his breath.

Underneath the display, a well-groomed man sat slumped in an enormous gold throne, playing with an elaborate rapier sword. His black hair was perfectly parted and his strong chin was closely shaven. He would have been quite handsome if it hadn't been for his crooked nose and bitter expression. It was Jake's uncle, Kear Cutler. A small impish-looking servant skulked beside the throne, craning his neck like a curious child.

"My lord," said the bearded trooper, kneeling. "These are the undertakers from outside the nebula."

Kear sat forward and raised a neatly plucked eyebrow. His charcoal-black eyes scanned the skull-shaped space helmets as the Space Dogs lined up in front of him. "It's been awhile since I visited the outside universe," he said. "But I don't recall undertakers dressing like that. What do you make of them, Grimble?"

"They look like space pirates to me, my lord," rasped the servant.

"We are indeed proud space pirate kin," admitted Granny Leatherhead, bowing her head. "At your service."

"How did you find Altus?" asked Kear, putting down his sword and rising from his throne.

"Amicus Kent revealed your location to us before he died," she lied.

The bearded trooper flinched at the mention of the old general.

"Did he now?" Kear sounded surprised.

"Fear not, your highness," said Granny Leatherhead. "Your secret is safe with us."

Kear snorted. "What makes you think that I would risk letting a bunch of spacejackers leave here alive? After all, dead pirates tell no tales."

Grimble laughed maliciously, but no one else seemed to find this funny.

Granny Leatherhead smiled modestly. "We've left some of our crew behind as insurance. If we don't return within two days, they will pass your coordinates to the Galactic Trade Corporation, who would love to get their drills into your crystal moons."

"You dare to blackmail me?" Kear's eyes bulged with anger.

"Forgive us, mighty ruler," she said. "All we seek is a small reward for bringing you these coffins—a little something to cover our costs."

"Ah yes, the coffins." Kear turned his attention to the three timber crates. "It's funny, they don't look expensive. Do you think it's acceptable to present the remains of an Altian leader in such a cheap casket?"

"It was our understanding that Andras Cutler was a traitor and he deserved nothing more than a wooden box," said Granny Leatherhead innocently.

"Ha, spoken like a true pirate." Kear's lips curled into a cruel smile. "I like you, one-eyed woman. You're well informed and you have no fear. You must also be very persuasive to get Amicus Kent to betray his planet."

"Indeed."

The bearded trooper tightened his grip on his rifle.

"Come, open these coffins," said Kear, rubbing his hands. "You have done Altus a great service. This will put an end to the conspiracy theories and uprisings. Now that I have the seal of Altus, no one will dare to question my authority again."

"Conspiracy theories?" inquired Granny Leatherhead. "Uprisings?"

"Yes, these are troubled times. There are some who believe my brother, Andras, and his son, Jake, will return to rule Altus. Their protests have caused me no end of problems. Here I am, trying to drag this planet out of the dark ages and all they do is complain. What else do they want? Fishing is more efficient, farming is more productive, and if it wasn't for me, lunar power would still be a dream."

"People can be so ungrateful."

"Ungrateful?" said Kear. "A wise person once told me if you can't make your subjects love you, then you should make them fear you. I've had to use fear to control this world and still my people turn against me. It's not as if I enjoy punishing the protesters. But all that will stop now that I have proof Andras is dead."

Granny Leatherhead signaled for her crew to open the first coffin.

"Who lies in this one?" asked Kear.

"Your nephew, Jake Cutler."

The lid was wrenched free and inside lay Jake, perfectly still with his arms crossed and the gold pendant resting on his chest. Strewn around his body were personal items, including the cutlass from Scargus. Kear leaned forward and examined the face of his nephew.

"I've not seen this boy since he was a toddler, but I can tell it's him. He has his father's nose and the family chin. Where has he been all these years?"

"We found him in the seventh solar system," said Granny Leatherhead. "Hiding on a planet called Remota."

Kear stooped lower to get a closer look.

"How did he die? There are no visible wounds or signs of poisoning. In fact, he looks rather healthy for a—"

"Hello, Uncle." Jake sat up and opened his eyes. "It's been a long time."

Kear jerked back, startled. "What's this?"

With lightning speed, Jake grabbed his cutlass and held it to Kear's throat, pressing the edge of the blade against his pampered skin.

"Nobody move," he yelled.

It took the troops a moment to realize what was happening, which was just long enough for the Space Dogs to crack open the other coffins, where Kella and Nanoo were hiding with more weapons. Granny Leatherhead snatched up her laser pistol and waved it in the air.

"You heard the lad. One false step and Uncle No Friends will have his bitter blood splattered over this throne."

None of the troops moved.

"How can this be?" Kear stared at his nephew in disbelief. "What happened to your eyes? Why are they sparkling?"

Jake stood up. "I've had these implants since I was two years old, thanks to you."

Kear glanced at the empty coffins. "I don't understand. Where are Andras and Amicus?"

"You sabotaged our ship." Jake's hand shook with anger. "Because of you, I've grown up without a father. Amicus Kent died a few days ago, but not before telling me who betrayed us. He was right—you wanted to claim Altus for yourself."

Kear pushed Jake's cutlass aside with his finger.

"How dare you point a sword at me?" he growled, his dark eyes twitching with anger. "Where's your evidence? I've committed no crime."

293

"Kear not speak truth," said Nanoo, holding up his homemade lie detector. "He guilty."

"Was it worth it, Uncle?" Jake placed the blade back against Kear's throat. "Were the last eleven years on that throne worth the lives of my father's crew?"

"Who do you think you are, boy?"

"I'm the rightful ruler of Altus," said Jake. "Which makes you . . . fired."

"Is that so?" Kear clenched his fists and shook with rage. "We'll see about that, you purple-eyed freak. The only way you'll take this planet is over my dead body."

"Don't tempt me," said Jake, stepping out of the coffin. "I might have been raised by cyber-monks, but I haven't taken their vows of peace."

"Guards!" roared Kear, frothing at the mouth in anger. "What are you waiting for? Kill them all."

Jake braced himself for the sound of laser fire, but none came. The troops remained in position, their rifles rested.

"Steady, Space Dogs," said Granny Leatherhead. "This fight is between Jake and his uncle."

"Guards?" Kear glared at his troops. "What's the meaning of this?"

The bearded trooper approached Jake, his every step traced by Granny Leatherhead's chunky pistol. He stopped and examined the glowing pendant.

"This isn't the first time that I've seen the seal of Altus, and its beauty has not faded," he said. "Are you really Jake Cutler, son of Andras Cutler?"

"Yes, I've returned to Altus to take my place as your rightful ruler and to make Kear Cutler pay for his crimes."

The bearded trooper considered these words before dropping onto one knee and saluting. "My name is Rex Kent, captain of the guard. Amicus Kent was my cousin. It's good to have you back, my lord. Your planet needs you."

"Thank you, Rex," said Jake, surprised. "Your cousin was a good man and a loyal servant of Altus."

"I never doubted it for a second. What are your orders, my lord?"

His orders? Jake wasn't ready for this question. All his energy had been focused on finding Altus. The whole room waited for him to speak, but his mind went blank. What should he say? He opened his mouth, hoping some words would come out.

"My orders . . ."

"Look out!" cried Kella.

While Jake was caught off guard, Kear used the opportunity to reach for his rapier.

"Mutiny," thundered Kear, swinging the blade at his nephew. "I'll put an end to this treachery once and for all."

Jake lifted his cutlass just in time to block the attack, but Kear lashed out again, clipping Jake's ear and drawing blood. Jake cried in pain and pulled away. This was it, his first real sword fight, and he was already losing. What had Scargus taught him about using a cutlass? It was all about movement and balance. Jake was smaller than his uncle, but he was also younger and faster.

"What's the matter, boy?" sneered Kear. "Missing your daddy?"

Fueled by anger, Jake leaped forward, his cutlass cutting and thrusting at his command. He released a combination of rapid strikes, like a crazed acrobat twisting and spinning, attacking with all his might. Kear struggled to fend off his nephew and jumped up onto the throne. Jake went to follow but instead caught a boot in the face.

"Take that, you little runt," snarled Kear.

Jake ignored the pain in his cheek and the warm blood trickling from his nose. They weren't important. Nothing was going to stop him from avenging his father. He circled his uncle, moving with pace and agility, his confidence growing with every strike. Kear scowled, but there was fear in his eyes.

"What's the matter, Uncle?" asked Jake. "Missing your guards?"

Adrenaline surged through Jake's veins. It was his time, his revenge, his victory. All eyes were on Jake and his uncle, which is why no one noticed Grimble slip from the crowd. The impish man pulled a two-way radio from his pocket and activated it.

"Help!" he rasped. "Pirates! Traitors! We're under attack. Send more troops!"

Jake's implants flickered.

"No!" he cried, as the sight of his uncle distorted before his eyes, leaving only static and shadows. "Not now!"

Jake cursed himself for not realizing the Altians would need to use old technology. Grimble's two-way radio had scrambled his vision. He staggered backward, swinging his sword at random.

Kear saw his chance and lunged, sinking his blade deep into his nephew's arm. Jake reeled in agony and dropped his cutlass, which clattered to the floor. He stood there, holding his wounded arm, blind and unarmed, waiting for his uncle to strike again.

"Never mind, nephew," sneered Kear. "At least we know your coffin fits."

Jake was angrier than he had ever been before. He was angry with himself, angry with his implants, and angry with Altian technology, but most of all he was angry with Kear Cutler. It had been eleven years since Kear betrayed his father, eleven years since their ship was destroyed, eleven years of not knowing who he was or where he came from. He had been through so much to find Altus, he was not going to give up now.

"No more!" he shouted at the shadow in front of him. "It ends here."

Jake dropped onto his knees and groped around on the floor where his cutlass had fallen. His fingers touched its familiar leather grip, which he seized with both hands. He threw himself forward, putting his entire weight behind the blow. His blade sliced through the air and connected with something metal, his uncle's sword, knocking it from his hand.

"Hey," cried Kear.

Jake pointed his cutlass directly at the shadow, trying to think of a single reason why he shouldn't run his sword through it. His vision cleared and his uncle appeared in front of him, cowering on the floor, nursing his wrist. Across the hall, Kella and Nanoo had Grimble pinned to the wall, his two-way radio smashed on the floor.

"But you're just a kid," said Kear.

"That's right, Kid Cutler."

Kear forced a nervous smile. "You wouldn't harm your old uncle, would you, Jakey?"

Jake raised his cutlass above his head. "You want to bet that throne on it?"

More Altians appeared in the doorway. The name Jake Cutler was spreading among the crowd. All of them looked astonished to see the thirteen-year-old boy and his gold pendant.

Jake kept an eye on Kear as he addressed the gathering crowd.

"As the rightful ruler of Altus, I order you to arrest this man for crimes of treason," he said, speaking with as much authority as he could muster. "Kear Cutler has betrayed his brother and his planet. Andras was on a mission to protect Altus when the Interstellar Navy attacked his ship. If it hadn't been for Kear sabotaging our weapons, my dad and his crew would still be here today."

"Yes, my lord." Rex signaled to his troops. "You heard him. Take Kear away and spread the word— Jake Cutler is back."

The Great Hall erupted with cheers and applause.

Kear's reign of terror was finally over. It was a historic moment, the day the boy ruler returned to Altus and defeated his uncle. The jubilant sounds washed over Jake like warm water. He was finally back where he belonged.

Chapter 26

The Protectorate

It had been a month since Jake had returned to Altus. Kear had been hauled off to prison by his own guards and Jake was in charge of a world he barely knew. News of his return had spread quickly and Altians traveled from all over the planet to Karmadon, hoping to catch a glimpse of their new leader and his heroic friends.

Over the last few weeks, Jake had been introduced to dozens of politicians, many of whom had been imprisoned for speaking out against Kear. Jake had used his new powers to release them. He had also met several distant relatives, who seemed nice enough, but they were little more than strangers to him.

Jake had found it difficult to know whom to trust. He had realized that he needed someone strong to support him, someone with inside knowledge who could stop him from making obvious mistakes. With this in mind, he had appointed Rex Kent as his top general and adviser. Rex's first suggestion was for Jake to ban two-way radios in order to protect his eyes.

While the Space Dogs enjoyed their hero status down in the city, Jake had moved into his old family mansion on the hill, not far from the Great Hall. It boasted white marble walls, huge windows, extensive grounds and a heated swimming pool. The house had been empty since his father left, because his uncle had chosen to build a much bigger mansion nearby. Kear Cutler had "borrowed" all of the luxury vehicles from the garage, leaving only an old hover-bike gathering dust in the corner.

Jake lay on a bed in one of the smaller rooms, studying his locket. The only other people in the mansion were Kella and Nanoo, who were staying on the far side of the building.

"Ah, there you are," said Kella, poking her head around the door. "I've been looking for you everywhere. What are you doing in here?"

Jake was lost in thought and it took him a moment to register the question.

"For the first time in my life, I felt the need to be alone," he said. "And this seemed like a good place."

"Here?"

"It was once my bedroom." Jake pointed to his name painted on the wall. "I don't remember sleeping here, but it feels sort of comforting."

"Do you want me to go?" she asked.

"No, it's okay."

Kella stepped farther into the room and looked around.

"It's nice in here," she said, and glanced out of the window. "Hey, there's an orchard down there."

"Yeah, I know. That must explain why I like apples so much." Jake held up his open locket. "It's the same window in the photo. My mom once sat where you're standing."

Kella walked over and perched on the edge of the bed. Her face was creased with concern, but before she could say anything, they were joined by Nanoo.

"Hi, guys," he said. "What up, Jake?"

Kella looked annoyed at Nanoo's lack of tact, but equally curious as to why Jake was hiding in his old bedroom.

"I found out that it's my birthday today," said Jake. "My *real* birthday."

"Why didn't you say something?" asked Kella. "We should have a party."

"It's okay, I don't feel much like celebrating."

Nanoo seemed to guess what was on Jake's mind.

"How is ruler of Altus going?"

"Terrible," said Jake. "I can't understand half of what the politicians are saying. It's like they're speaking another language. Who knew politics was so complicated?"

"And boring?"

"Uh-huh. It's not half as exciting as being a space pirate, but I have to make up for my uncle's mistakes."

"Are you sure that's what you want?" asked Kella.

"You think I'm too young, don't you?" said Jake. "Why would anyone listen to me?"

"Garbish." Nanoo pointed at the gold pendant. "You born to lead. It in your blood."

"He's right," said Kella. "There have been loads of child rulers in the history of the galaxy. You're not the first and I doubt you'll be the last."

"Would you follow me?"

Nanoo laughed. "We have already, Jake, across solar system and back."

Jake stood up and surveyed the orchard. "I just don't want to ruin my dad's memory."

"From what we've been hearing, he was a great man," said Kella.

"You find photo of him?" asked Nanoo.

"No, not yet. It's as though Kear wanted to wipe out any sign that he ever existed. How could someone hate their own brother that much?"

"You know what they say." Kella joined Jake by the window. "You can choose your friends, but not your family."

Jake sighed. "For as long as I can remember, I wanted to know who I was and where I was from, but now that I know, I don't feel any different."

"Maybe what matters is not who you were or where you came from," said Kella. "But who you are now and where you want to be."

"I thought that I belonged here on Altus, but it means nothing without my parents." Jake looked beyond the orchard to the roof of the Great Hall. "They want to put up a gold statue of my dad, but I won't let them."

"Why not?" asked Nanoo.

Jake rested his forehead on the glass. "Because you only put up statues of dead people, and I'm not ready to accept that my dad is gone."

Kella went to put her arm around him, when Jake heard the front door close. He spun around.

"Callidus?"

"I doubt it," she said. "He's been back on the *Dark Horse* since Kear was arrested. I think he's helping Scargus and Manik to repair the ship. For someone who spent years searching for Altus, he doesn't seem very happy to be here."

Nanoo lowered his voice. "Nichelle reckon Callidus work on way to tow crystal moon through Tego Nebula."

"I'd like to see him try," said Jake. "I expect he's planning his next adventure. It's not like there's anything to keep him here now."

"Hello?" called out a familiar voice. "Anyone home?"

"It's Rex." Jake went to greet his general, leaving Kella and Nanoo in the bedroom.

"Ah, there you are," said Rex, climbing the stairs. "My lord, you've been summoned to see the Protectorate."

"The what?"

"The Protectorate. It's a council of elders entrusted with keeping Altus a secret. Their job is to protect this world and its inhabitants from outsiders."

"Outsiders? You mean like my friends."

"I mean anyone who poses a threat to this planet," said Rex. "Your friends may not be dangerous people, but can they keep a secret? What if they were captured and tortured? Would they reveal our location? What if someone offered them money or power in exchange for information? Would they resist temptation? It's up to the Protectorate to decide who can or cannot be trusted to leave this world."

"Is that not my decision, as ruler?"

"No. Matters of planetary security are too important to be left up to one person. Therefore the Protectorate have the power to overrule you. Not even your uncle would dare to oppose them."

"But what if they decide my friends can't be trusted? How do I tell Kella and Nanoo that they can never go home?" Jake paced the floor. "The others won't be happy about this either. I know you can't trust a space pirate, or a fortune seeker, but can't we make them swear an oath or something?"

"The Protectorate's decision is final," said Rex. "We know the Galactic Trade Corporation is searching for our crystal moons. They would mine them to the core, which would upset the gravitational balance and destroy Altus."

Rex had a point, but Jake didn't like the sound of this secret council. None of the crew had said they were ready to leave yet, though he doubted they wanted to stay forever. Jake asked the general to wait downstairs while he changed into more formal clothes. He rushed back into the bedroom and closed the door.

"What going on?" asked Nanoo.

"I don't have much time," whispered Jake, ripping off his shirt and pants. "I've been summoned to a secret council. They want to stop you and the others from leaving Altus. Wait until I've gone and then gather everyone back at the ship. Tell the crew to prepare for an emergency launch."

"What about you?" asked Kella.

"Don't worry about me." Jake pulled on a crisp Altian uniform, complete with tassels, stripes, and a customized sheath for his cutlass. "I'll let you know once a decision has been reached."

"Okay," said Nanoo. "We spread word."

Kella handed Jake his sword. "You certainly look like a ruler in that outfit. I can't believe you're the same boy I met at Papa Don's."

It was early evening and the crystal moons were setting as Rex Kent escorted Jake through the orchard to the Great Hall. Instead of using the main entrance, they walked around the side to a small wooden door. Rex used a long key to open a rusty lock and left to attend to urgent military business. Jake entered alone and descended a stone staircase to a candlelit room below.

"Greetings, Jake Cutler," said a voice in the gloom.

Jake's eyes adjusted to the low lighting. He made out twelve people sitting around a large circular table, each of them wrapped in a hooded crimson robe and wearing a glowing crystal medallion.

"You must be the Protectorate."

"Yes, that's correct." The woman who spoke looked twice as old as Granny Leatherhead. "We've been selected as the wisest of the Altians to keep this planet safe."

"It's a great honor to be chosen," said another woman, squinting at Jake with faded, bloodshot eyes. "The council has been in place since the first refugees founded Karmadon city. We feared that Kear Cutler would sell us out to the Galactic Trade Corporation, but your return has prevented any such plot."

"Refugees?" Jake was confused. "I thought Altus was discovered by explorers."

"Not quite," said one of the oldest men. "Captain Alyus Don was on the run from the Interstellar Navy. His ship was full of outcasts from Zerost, their families slaughtered by naval troops. In desperation, the crew hid inside the Tego Nebula, which is when they stumbled across Altus. He believed that Altus was a reward for him and his crew, a gift from the universe to make amends for their hardship."

"But that means . . ." Jake's brain took a few seconds to catch up. "I must be a descendant of Zerost, the same as Granny Leatherhead. My ancestors were space pirates."

"Yes, but that doesn't mean we can trust your

shipmates to keep our location a secret, whether on purpose or by accident." The old man sat back in his chair. "It has already been decided—they can never leave Altus."

"No, you're wrong," said Jake. "We can trust them."

"How can you be so sure?" asked the woman with bloodshot eyes. "Are you prepared to risk the entire planet?"

"It's not like I want them to go." Jake approached the table. "But they are my friends and I owe them my life, which is why they must be allowed to choose for themselves."

"I'm sorry, but it's too late," said the old man. "General Kent is on his way to seize the pirate ship."

"What!"

Jake turned his back on the Protectorate and sprinted up the stone staircase. He had to warn his friends. As far as he was concerned, they had earned their freedom by helping to save Altus. He had to get to the *Dark Horse* before Rex.

Ignoring the outcry below, Jake grabbed the door handle and turned it, but the door refused to open. It was old and probably stuck, he told himself. He rammed it hard with his shoulder.

"Ouch!" Jake bounced off the wooden surface.

He was trapped.

Desperate to escape, he unsheathed his cutlass and hacked furiously at the old timber, but the door was too thick and his sword barely made a mark. Jake's speed meant nothing, when it was strength that he needed.

"Help," he cried. "Let me out."

It was pointless. Who would hear him?

"Hello?" called a voice on the other side. "Hold on. The door's blocked."

Jake could hear something heavy being dragged along the ground. The handle turned and the door swung open. Two figures stood in the darkness. Jake held up his cutlass, ready to defend himself.

"What's going on?" asked one of them.

"Why door barricaded?" asked the other.

"Kella? Nanoo? Is that you?" Jake lowered his sword. "What are you doing here?"

"We couldn't go without knowing you were okay," said Kella.

"What about the others?" asked Jake.

"It okay," said Nanoo. "They wait on ship."

Jake led Kella and Nanoo quickly away from the Great Hall and back toward his family's mansion. Only the ruby moon remained in the sky, bathing the city in bloodred light.

"I'm glad to see you guys," he said, as they hurried through the orchard. "But we've got to get you off the planet, before it's too late."

"How are we going to do that?" asked Kella. "The ship is miles away."

Jake stopped outside the garage. "Have either of you ever ridden a hover-bike?"

Kella and Nanoo opened the wide metal doors, while Jake fetched the hover-bike key from inside the mansion. By the time he returned, they had dragged out the dusty old contraption, which looked like a giant hair dryer resting on an upside-down bathtub. Jake swung his leg over the cracked leather seat and slipped the key into the ignition. He gripped the handlebars and kicked down on the starter lever, causing brown smoke to spew out of the exhaust pipes with a bang. The engine rattled a few times and fell silent.

"I thinking no one ride bike for long time," said Nanoo. "It not even lunar powered."

"Are you sure you know what you're doing?" asked Kella.

"Yes, of course," said Jake. "A friend of mine on Remota used to let me ride her hover-bike. It's our only hope of beating Rex back to the *Dark Horse*."

"Give another try," suggested Nanoo.

Jake placed his foot on the starter lever and paused. There were voices and footsteps coming from the Great Hall.

"Altian troops," said Kella, her eyes as wide as palm grenades.

Jake kicked down hard and the engine rumbled promisingly for a few seconds, before cutting out again. The voices drew closer and shapes could be seen moving between the apple trees.

"Hurry," said Nanoo.

Jake stamped on the starter lever with his entire weight. "Come on, start!"

The hover-bike roared to life, emitting further bangs and clouds of brown smoke.

"Quick, get on!" he shouted, revving the engine and blasting the ground with high-pressured air.

Kella and Nanoo climbed onto the rear and held on tight. The motors whined as the hover-bike lifted off the ground and wobbled in the air. Jake saw several armed figures emerging from the trees. He squeezed the accelerator and the bike shot forward, speeding through the open gates and onto the road.

"More troops," warned Nanoo, spotting two maroon vehicles.

Jake swerved the hover-bike off the road and down the side of the hill, parting the grass as they hurtled toward the city below. His fast reactions were tested to their limits as he wrestled with the handle-bars, struggling to control the bike, while the others held on for their lives.

"Watch out for that tree," screamed Kella. "And that bush . . . and those vehicles!"

The hover-bike was heading straight for a busy street at the bottom of the hill, and there was no way it was going to stop in time.

Chapter 27

A Difficult Decision

Jake slammed on the brakes and slid the hover-bike sideways onto the busy street, tucking it between two large green buses and narrowly avoiding a hover-truck coming the other way. He squeezed the accelerator and rode the old machine through traffic, weaving dangerously around cars and lorries. Kella tightened her grip around his waist as they reached the main road out of Karmadon.

"I didn't know you could ride like that," she said.

"Neither did I." Jake shifted up a gear. "Hold on. We're approaching the city gates."

The guards had stopped traffic and were closing the tall iron gates, which looked like huge metal jaws clamping shut. It was the only way out of Karmadon and the walls were too high to jump, even for a hover-bike. Jake pulled hard on the accelerator and raced toward the narrowing gap.

"Halt," commanded the guard, standing in the road.

Jake ignored him and stayed on course, approaching the gates at breakneck speed. The guard dived to the ground at the last second and the hover-bike flew over his head. It scraped through the remaining gap in a shower of sparks, losing both wing mirrors and half its faded paintwork.

"Magnifty!" cheered Nanoo, as they reached the other side.

"That was close," said Jake, steering the hover-bike across a lake and through a cluster of trees. "From now on, I'll avoid the roads."

"Good idea," agreed Kella. "But how are we going to find the *Dark Horse*?"

"Not easy," said Nanoo. "We need handheld computer to find fastest route."

"You mean like this one?" Jake pulled a small package from inside his uniform and passed it back to Nanoo. "I grabbed it from the mansion. I've had it adjusted to work inside the nebula cloud."

Nanoo activated the device and squinted at its bright display. He slid his fingers over the screen, using the device to scan the area and create a map, while Jake did his best to keep the hover-bike steady.

"I just hope we have enough fuel to get there," said Kella, tapping the tank with her heel.

Nanoo guided them through picturesque meadows and patches of woodland until they reached a narrow river that led back to the farm. Jake couldn't help but admire the beauty of Altus, even at night, with its swaying grass and giant trees. He followed the course of the river, flying inches above its surface, letting the water spray his face.

"How much farther?" asked Kella.

Nanoo checked their position. "It not long, but there is low bridge ahead."

"No problem," said Jake. "We'll go around it."

The hover-bike left the water and soared along the muddy riverbank, sending animals scurrying into the trees and bushes. The bridge appeared in the distance, cast in shadows.

"What's that sitting on top of it?" asked Kella.

Jake stared at the large shape. Was it moving? He hit the brakes and brought the hover-bike to a halt, but it was too late. Headlights flooded the riverbank, ensnaring the three of them like startled rabbits. A few yards away a maroon hover-tank floated above the bridge, its hull lined with hexagonal panels and its twin gun barrels pointed directly at them.

"What we do now?" whispered Nanoo.

"I don't know," said Jake, noticing more armored vehicles lined up and down the road.

A small hatch popped open on the tank turret and a bearded face emerged.

"Hello, Jake," said Rex Kent. "I had a feeling the Protectorate wouldn't hold you for long."

"You betrayed me," said Jake angrily. "I thought we were friends."

"We are," insisted Rex, taken aback. "I've been your friend and faithful servant since the day you were born."

"Prove it," said Jake. "Leave the *Dark Horse* alone."

Rex switched to his official tone. "I'm sorry, my lord, but I cannot disobey a direct order from the Protectorate, whatever my personal feelings."

"But it's not fair. The Space Dogs helped to free Altus from my uncle. Doesn't that count for anything?"

Rex climbed down from the hover-tank. "If it were up to me, I would give them all medals, but it's not my decision."

"And what about Kella and Nanoo?" asked Jake. "They need to find their own people. Are you going to stop them from leaving?"

Rex shook his head. "We've only been instructed to detain the space pirates."

"Well, that includes me," said Jake. "I'm part of the crew. Keep me and let the others go."

Rex watched the old hover-bike cough and

sputter on the riverbank. Jake could sense the conflict inside the bearded general, torn between his duty and his heart.

"I was only a cadet when your father left Altus," said Rex. "He was a great man and a valiant leader."

"He still is," insisted Jake. "Andras Cutler is still alive as far as I'm concerned."

"Listen," said Rex quietly. "I may not be able to refuse the Protectorate, but they didn't say how quickly I had to carry out their orders. If you ask me, my troops aren't used to all this excitement and they could do with a rest."

"What are you saying?"

"I'll give you a five-minute head start." Rex winked at Jake. "Now go, before I change my mind."

Was this another trick? Jake edged the hover-bike off the riverbank and onto the bridge. There was no point avoiding the roads now.

"Thank you, Rex. If anything happens to me, I want you to look after Altus until my dad returns."

"Yes, my lord."

Jake saluted his top general and rode off into the night with Kella and Nanoo. His friends weren't free yet, but at least Rex had bought them some time. Not wasting a second, Jake opened up the throttle and raced toward the nearby farmland.

A few minutes later, Nanoo tapped him on the shoulder and waved the handheld computer. "According to device, we should see *Dark Horse* now."

"Where?" Kella's head shot from side to side. "I can only see fields."

Jake slowed the hover-bike and stared into the darkness, unable to spot anything shaped like a ship. Had the Space Dogs left already?

"There is it!" cried Nanoo, pointing.

Jake recognized the cargo hauler's familiar silhouette nestled between two farm buildings, its porthole windows glowing with warm amber light. He steered the hover-bike off the road, over a low hedge and across a field toward it. As they drew close, he noticed something resembling a barn roof positioned behind the ship. It looked as though Scargus and Manik had managed to construct a launchpad, with a little help from their farmer friends.

With no time to park, Jake rode straight up the loading ramp and into the cargo hold, where he ditched the bike. The crew were waiting impatiently in the dining area on the first deck. It was the first time that Jake had seen Callidus in weeks and the fortune seeker appeared rough, as though he had forgotten how to sleep and shave.

"Well?" demanded Granny Leatherhead, wearing hexagonal moon glasses. "What's all this about? It had better be important, because I was watching the moon set on a beach quite literally made of golden sand."

"They don't want you to leave Altus," said Jake.

"That's very flattering," she croaked. "But we can't hide here forever waiting for the Interstellar Navy to find us. What would we do? Join the Altian planetary guard? No offense, your rulership, but we're not used to taking orders and I would look terrible in a maroon uniform. No, I'm afraid we'll have to face the outside universe sooner or later."

"You don't understand," said Kella. "Troops are on their way to seize the ship."

"Troops!" Nichelle exclaimed.

"Yes, and hover-tank," said Nanoo.

"Hey, that's no way to treat their saviors," objected Capio. "I knew this planet was too good to be true."

The other shipmates expressed their disapproval. Nobody wanted to be held against their will, not even in paradise.

"We can't leave yet," said Granny Leatherhead, folding her arms. "What about our reward?"

"There's no time," insisted Jake.

"But we'll have nothing without those crystals," said Farid.

"We'll have our freedom." Callidus sounded gruff. "How much is that worth?"

Granny Leatherhead let out a tirade of curses and ordered the crew to prepare for launch.

"I'll delay the troops as long as I can," said Jake. "When you take off, head straight for the nebula. Altus has a small fleet of ships that haven't been used in years, but they're still armed and spaceworthy."

"Won't you get into trouble?" asked Kella.

"It's okay." Jake stood tall in his Altian uniform. "I'm always in trouble. Just promise me that you'll keep Altus a secret."

"You're a good lad, Jake." Granny Leatherhead fetched a small piece of cloth from her pocket and stuffed it in his hand. "Here, this is for you."

It was a pirate patch, like the ones the crew wore on their combat suits, with an illustration of the *Dark Horse* fighting the ISS *Colossus* over the black hole. Jake read the words *Battle of the Black Hole* underneath. It was only a piece of cloth, but it meant more to him than all the crystals in the universe.

"Thank you," he said. "Where in Zerost did you get it?"

"I made it from an old blanket."

"You?"

"Yes. I have a talent for embroidery," she croaked.

"But if you tell anyone, I'll cut out your tongue and call you a liar."

Jake hugged the old captain and turned to find Callidus blocking his exit.

"I'm sorry it has to end like this," said the fortune seeker. "But to be honest, I'll be glad to leave Altus."

"Why?" asked Jake. "I thought it was just how you imagined."

"It is," said Callidus. "And that's the problem. It's not easy coming face-to-face with your dreams. I fell in love with the idea of Altus, and this place is a little too real for me. I've achieved what I set out to do, and now it's time to move on to a new challenge."

"Will I ever see you again?"

"I hope so." Callidus cracked a smile. "You owe me a crate of crystals."

"Thanks for bringing me home. I don't know what would have happened if you hadn't helped me on Remota. You believed in me when it counted and I won't ever forget that."

"Good," said Callidus, stepping aside. "Because none of us will forget purple-eyed Jake Cutler, the ruler of Altus. Just do me a favor: keep an eye on the stars and stay out of trouble."

The crew called out their good-byes as Jake made

his way to the hatch, where Kella and Nanoo were waiting anxiously.

"It doesn't feel right leaving you like this," said Kella. "Not after everything we've been through together."

"We stay with Jake," said Nanoo. "Help you to run planet."

Jake hated the thought of Kella and Nanoo leaving, but it would be unfair to keep them on Altus.

"No," he said firmly. "You have your own people to find. Kella, your parents will be worried sick and your sister needs you. What about your Novu engine, Nanoo? It's a long way back to Taan-Centaur."

"So this is good-bye?" Kella's voice wavered.

Jake nodded. "Yeah, I guess so."

"It sad, but friends always," said Nanoo, placing a hand on Jake's shoulder.

"We'll never forget you." Kella embraced him, her emerald-green eyes glistening with tears. "I hope you find your father."

Jake hadn't realized how much he would miss his friends until that moment. He wanted to tell them what they meant to him and how he wanted to go with them more than anything, but his voice seemed to get stuck in his throat. All he could manage were a few hoarse words.

"I'll see you around."

He hurried down the metal staircase, his feet scuffing the steps for the last time. With less than a minute to go, he stopped in the cargo hold to compose himself. The smell of grease and engine oil reminded him of the first time he had entered the ship. Was that only a few months ago? His eyes drifted to the rusting wall and the names scratched into the metal surface.

"Proud space pirate kin," he whispered.

Unsheathing his cutlass, he used the tip of the blade to carve his name below the others.

"Good-bye, Kid Cutler," he said, stepping back. "It was fun while it lasted."

The engine fired up and Jake headed down the loading ramp to wait for Rex. As he stood beneath the ship, listening to the familiar clunking sounds above him, he started to question his actions. What was he doing? After everything his friends had done for him, he was letting them face the Interstellar Navy alone. Jake didn't want to abandon his shipmates, but he was duty-bound to serve Altus.

In a moment, the *Dark Horse* would blast into the sky and disappear through the Tego Nebula, never to be seen again. What had Kella said about Jake finding his father? How could he search for someone if he didn't go anywhere? And what about the promise he had made to Kella and Nanoo? How could he help them from his mansion?

Jake held the gold pendant in one hand and the pirate patch in the other, as though trying to weigh up two different futures. Whether he liked it or not, he had to choose between his friends and his home planet.

Farid appeared at the top of the loading ramp.

"You had better stand clear," he shouted. "We're about to take off."

At the edge of the field, a row of bright lights floated toward him. Jake could make out the bulky shape of the hover-tank, flanked by four maroon trucks. He wondered if the Protectorate would punish him for helping his shipmates to escape, but then he realized it didn't matter. In fact, nothing would matter once his friends had left.

It came down to one question: who did he want to be the most, Jake Cutler the boy ruler, or Kid Cutler the space pirate?

There was no contest.

"Wait!" he shouted, leaping onto the closing ramp. "I'm coming with you."

Jake sprinted past Farid, through the cargo hold, along the corridor, and into the guest quarters. He leaped onto his old bunk and strapped himself in.

"Jake?" exclaimed Capio, sitting up. "I thought you were staying behind."

"Never trust a space pirate," said Jake.

"What changed your mind?" asked Callidus.

"I've worked it out, Cal. I know who I am and where I want to be. I'm Kid Cutler and I want to be here, aboard the *Dark Horse* with my friends, not in some mansion surrounded by advisers and politicians."

"Good lad," said Capio.

"What about Altus?" asked Callidus.

"It'll have to survive without me," said Jake. "What do I know about running a planet? Rex Kent can keep an eye on things until I return with my father, Andras, the true ruler of Altus."

Jake lay flat on his bunk, his heart racing. Any second now, the crew would switch the engine to full throttle and release the thrusters. Any second now, the *Dark Horse* would rise up into the sky. Any second now, they would head into outer space in search of new adventures. Jake didn't know if his father was waiting for him in the stars, but he was determined to find out.